# THE VENCELLO

S. Amaranthine

www.thevencello.com



The Vencello/ S. Amaranthine -- 1st ed.
ISBN 978-0-9963229-2-8

*Acknowledgments*

Thank you to my two dolphin friends, whose real names I will never know. You are my true inspirations. I love you and think of you often. I am writing this book for you.

Thank you to my daughters. I love you more than anything else, ever. I am so proud of you. Like everything else I do, I am writing the trilogy for you.

Thank you to my grandchildren. You are not born yet and I may never know your names either. But I'm not going to wait for your birth to start loving you. I already do and I think of you often. I am writing this book for you too.

Thank you Wenda Pichardo. I so appreciate your taking time to read the early draft of this book and your valuable feedback. You cared about it much more than I did then.

Thank you Dave Ellerhorst for your support, which I have come to rely on for so much.

A HUGE thank you to Jenn Stark for enthusiastic and professional feedback. You are an inspiration and a true talent!

Thank you Liz Bemis of Bemis Promotions for your graphic art talent in putting the cover together.

Thank you to Heather Osborn for professional editing.

Thank you to all of those unsung hard working mothers and grandmothers—the orca matriarchs. I know what you know—it's all about love and family.

Thank you to all of the Masters of the Ocean for your big-brain inspiration—whatever universe you happen to be in.

# PROLOGUE

*You've asked the question, 'what is the Vencello'?*

Here is a short answer—that was the name of a singing game my grandmother taught me. Always singing, ours was a world of perpetual music. There could be no understanding without it. This was one of her easier games, a riddle of sorts.

*Imagine I have hands. Imagine I have a ball, a sphere, in one of them. A ball was your first toy. A ball is a* part *of the scene we are imagining. That is, it is as a* particle, *a distinct piece of a larger whole, and can therefore be first. Time was and is also yours to play with, but cannot first, because there is no beginning or end to time. Time is as a* wave. *We may look at the scene and conclude the wave contains the particle; the ball within an endless ocean. The ocean expands around the scene you imagine, around you wherever you will go and where I have been. You may think of yourself as an object, a particle as distinct as the ball, stuck in time. What if you could pull yourself away from time, as if the wave was conceptually containable, a particle itself? Imagine I have time in my other hand. Clear your mind, close your eyes and imagine it right in front of you and then open your eyes and look at it. What does it look like?*

Grandmother hoped this would keep me quietly busy while she scanned the surroundings for prey. I loved her so and our lessons together. It seemed that one always included developing patience. Remaining quiet was difficult when I had her all to myself. But I was to learn more from her than song and survival. Before she would start the next game I had to explain my answer to the first. I would feign deep thought, a good joke in itself because we both knew I could conceal nothing from her, but then gave the same answer, "It would look like a ball". Then she would always say, "You don't look like a ball to me!"

One time I looked at her hard when she asked the question, 'What does it look like?' I scanned her eye and the complex mystery behind it. I answered instead, "A brain." She liked that answer very much. With her songs, she helped me to understand our bond, what we were; mortal particles, immortal wave. We were unique individuals but were also unmistakably combined as one—musician(s), space explorer(s), time traveler(s), and powerful creator(s).

Now for a longer answer.

# CHAPTER ONE: DAY ONE

## Human: DELORA

**Delora's personal field journal**:

*Akenehi's clan suffered a horrific loss today. I know this pod family. She is the senior female, the matriarch, a grandmother and my friend. She leads her family with great affection, patience, superior cunning and predatory skills. We have developed an exceptional bond. We have even established a few shared whistle sounds associated with our friendly encounters. There is no way I could have made the intimate observations I have without her permission, her acceptance of my presence. I owe so much to her. I thought I'd been witness to as much as any human would be to their everyday natural lives—all thanks to Akenehi. But nothing could have prepared me for this. Today, I witnessed Akenehi's son, Hototo, suffer a fatal injury as a result of a botched shark hunt.*

*At age 16, he already weighed an estimated 10 tons, had an impressively tall dorsal fin with a distinctive double notch near his body, handsome crisp black and white markings, and I imagine even among his own family pod, he was considered an outstanding and beautiful specimen of his species. Hototo was not Akenehi's first or only son, but he appeared to be her favorite. His hormones had been obviously elevated as of late and he had been outrageous and daring in his challenges to other males, and even more so in his advances to a particular young female in another pod. As a young male Orca, he had sometimes challenged and appeared victorious, but more often had been bitten, slashed, rammed and raked. This year brought an ocean swell of change growing in him—greater size and strength and his desire to stage offensives of his own.*

*Today, the family was observed in very close proximity to at least one Great White shark. I wasn't sure if they were hunting it, fleeing from it, or if it was mere coincidence. It wasn't known until very recently that they could hunt and kill these formidable beasts until an Orca was observed holding a Great White in its jaws. Apparently, an Orca may kill a Great White by practiced approach and grasp behaviors so that the shark is held upside down firmly in the jaws. Turning the shark in this position renders it immobile and the Orca then grips the shark in its mouth and swims with it until the shark dies. Until today, I had not personally witnessed it. The capture and subduing of a large, in-its-prime Great White would not only provide food for the family but would undoubtedly demonstrate the successful skills of a great hunter. I'm fairly positive, in hindsight; Hototo was leading the hunt for the shark and was closing in for the kill.*

*I know this pod had successfully hunted Great Whites before, based on reports from local fishermen, so I can only imagine how or why Hototo made his fatal error. Perhaps he was sick, or not experienced enough with this particular prey.*

*I don't know if Orcas have medical skills or even a sort of scientific knowledge. I like to think they do. How else could they have survived so long is such an unforgiving, unprotected environment? There's nothing I could have done. I just know he was dying. The recording was so horrible to play back, so frantic, it sounded like they knew it too. There is no way he could survive that amount of blood loss. Akenehi wasted no time getting her family out of the area. I'm sure she anticipated a shark feeding frenzy if they didn't move. Akenehi and the family headed out, supporting Hototo between them. He was still visible at the surface when I lost sight of them.*

*I feel so much pity for all of them. I bring Alvar along with me often, and Akenehi has always shown a keen interest in him. I believe the Orca matriarch senses he is my son. And now I saw her son fatally injured. I'm so re-*

*lieved Alvar wasn't out here today. It was absolutely the worst thing I've ever seen.*

Alvar was Delora's only child. The events of the day left her thinking of him. Without doubt, he was her first, her last, and for all eternity, her favorite of all things. Alvar, at age 16, he already possessed a tall, strong, athletic physique, and more importantly, an extraordinary intelligence. But the characteristics she held most dear were his sweetness and an increasingly sharp wit. Of all of the things she has done, her making of this person was her magnum opus; unquestionable proof of her ability to do something great. Delora's heart broke for Akenehi's loss, and she pushed thoughts of how she would feel in the same situation right out of her mind. It was too unbearable to even consider. The possibility of such a thing was making her nauseous.

She closed her journal entry. It sounded rambling and emotional, and that wouldn't do. Colleagues might one day read it. She decided to edit it when she had regained her composure. She couldn't possibly note how she should have jumped in and helped, should have been closer. She cursed her human form, slow and ineffective in the water, deaf and dumb to most of what the clan communicated amongst themselves. She was useless to them. The clan must know that now. It was too cold and she preferred the warmth her dry gear and outerwear provided, rather than the usual dive and swim. Entry done, she began preparations for the trip back to land. The day's events had demanded extended recording and meticulous note taking and finally she was satisfied with her data collection. It was much later than usual as she finally started up the motor and headed to land and home.

Delora was born a typical healthy human female. None of her family was athletic but when Delora was first placed in a pool as a young child she took naturally to water. Her parents were not swimmers and her mother was even afraid of water. Delora taught herself within minutes how to come up to the air, hold her breath and swim happily underwater, then surface for breath again. It amazed her father, who soon after put a pool in their backyard. That pool was the only kindness she could really recall from him, but it was an incredibly wonderful gift and it profoundly impacted her life. In the water she felt enjoyment and comfort. Not so much outside of it. She swam as often as she could, but did not look super athletic. She looked like an average human female but could swim better than any of them. When she said she could have jumped in the ocean and helped an injured Orca, she almost believed it.

She was spending the last of her inheritance on her cetacean research. Because she was self- funded she didn't answer to anyone directing her daily activity or schedule. As far as Delora's goals went, she had achieved them. She was able to keep a nice sized, mechanically sound boat with a small sleeping area, research set-up and storage for her acoustic equipment, and supplies enough for an extended period out in open water. She had published papers on Orca vocalizations and behavior. She was known in the area and left to do her work largely unquestioned and unbothered. This all afforded her the solitude she preferred and the freedom to explore hypotheses at the most opportune moments as they presented themselves out at sea.

Alvar was her cetacean behavior research assistant. He genuinely wanted to share her work with her. If it were left to him he wouldn't attend school at all. He preferred the ocean and the company of the Orcas. He was just like his mother in that respect. She was incredibly proud of his intuitive brilliance about Orca behavior and his ability to hold their interest and company, which was unprecedented. He was more than her son and research assistant. He was an invaluable muse. Alvar didn't hesitate when she asked if he wanted to move to the seaside with her to live this life, it was definitely "Yes!" Alvar imagined he would water ski, scuba dive and hang out with the Orcas in their own private research paradise. That was pretty much how it had turned out so far, when he wasn't getting his brains bored out at school.

Alvar did not know his father. He'd never met him. Delora named Alvar after his father's nickname, which meant elf warrior. Delora and he had had a very short but productive relationship overseas. She was only 19 and had traveled there for a couple of weeks, protesting dolphin and whale slaughters that were occurring throughout the world. They literally bumped into each other while standing side by side in a close crowd. They were kindred spirits for the cause, and that was enough for her at the time. She actually knew very little about him.

A euphoric political zeal in combination with their youth and mutual attraction resulted in Alvar. When Delora returned home and discovered she was pregnant, he had already left the hostel he had been staying in, leaving no forwarding information and no means to locate him. That was a part in the story she had not shared with Alvar until very recently. That had to wait until he was old enough to understand about making stupid mistakes and being responsible for consequences. In every telling of the story, she emphatically reiterated that she had absolutely no regrets. Alvar was the best thing that ever happened to her.

**Human: ALVAR and JOHNNY**

Among his peers, Alvar was increasingly perceived as different. He spent so much time with his mother and the Orca pod that his socialization was affected. Some called him names meant to insult, such as momma's boy. He knew that would never be an insult to an Orca and for that reason Alvar was secretly proud when he was called that. It was true anyway; he loved his mother very much. He was increasingly protective of his female schoolmates, especially when they were subjected to unwanted groping in crowded hallways and insulting sexual comments. His challenges to offending males were drawing the admiration of many classmates and the intense hatred of a few of the perpetrators. Over the course of such challenges only one had resulted in an actual shoving match, and Alvar won, but it was the greatest attention getter of all.

One small group of harassers and bullies, Guy, Jacob and Johnny, all seniors, noticed Alvar's victory and chose him as their victim. Hoping Alvar would intervene; they cornered a female at the locker next to his and began to cruelly taunt her appearance. She did a fine job of defending herself but she was one against three and they surrounded her. Alvar was also their target and he knew it plainly. Not only were the three mean, they were poor actors. When they made their move to fondle her, Alvar made his. He was strong and brave, true to his name. Alvar made a terrible victim. They quickly regretted their choice.

Guy, the most ruthless bully in school, in a crowded hallway, was eloquently humiliated and easily put into submission. Alvar, standing tall and increasingly handsome to everyone present, pointed to Jacob and Johnny with a smile and terrifying poise and named Guy the most pathetic coward in the school. Guy was weak and knew it, hence the show, complete with required backup of his two equally needy mates. A teacher was closing in to intervene. The crowd that had gathered in hopes of a fight were disappointed and quickly headed to class. Alvar would achieve a temporary rock-star status with his fellow students. But after that public display Guy intended to regain his reputation.

Walking home alone from school on the very same day that Delora witnessed Hototo's violent death, Alvar saw the three bullies ahead, waiting for him. Guy wanted to do the honor of kicking Alvar's ass personally. Jacob was to help hold Alvar while he did so and join in if desired. Johnny was made the lookout.

Rather than turn and run, Alvar felt a surge of adrenaline and power at the thought of physically punishing these guys. He imaged the satisfying yield of facial flesh as his fist made solid contact. As he approached and did the math, he could almost hear his mother, pleading, ordering him to run. He figured she would be upset with him. He had been called into the headmaster's office recently and promised her he wouldn't get into a second fight. She reminded him he had a bright future; one that a record of fighting would likely destroy. He knew he was outnumbered, but not by much. Further he was quick, in great physical shape and righteous. If he ran now he would be humiliated and might even be running until graduation, perhaps his whole life. He ignored her. His step quickened towards the waiting three and his breathing increased. He even imagined he had a tall straight Orca dorsal fin, threatening and breaking surface water as he approached. Images of the power of Hototo and other adult male Orcas swam before him. He couldn't lose. This fight, and it would be *one hell* of a fight, would go his way.

Alvar had miscalculated. Guy and Jacob isolated Alvar, immobilized him after much effort and then proceeded to punch and kick him well past the point where he was down and no longer fighting back. They were vicious, mean and cowardly.

Except maybe Johnny. On Alvar's first day as a new student Johnny had eaten lunch with him. They hit it off immediately as they had a mutual interest in boats. Alvar's mother and Johnny's' brother both had one. They spent their conversation comparing models and motors. Johnny had hoped they could be friends. He soon realized that belonging to Guy's group made that unlikely. Guy hated Alvar and he enforced his will on his cronies. Johnny was weak in spirit.

Now Johnny had his back turned to them but clearly heard them beat Alvar as he stood watch. He wondered what Guy had meant by "teach him a lesson" and just how far Guy had intended to take this. This was starting to make Johnny physically sick. He decided it was time to find new friends. He was trying to muster the courage to stand up to Guy when he heard a sickening crunch and at that point he couldn't stand by any longer. He turned toward the brawl to see Guy's blood-smeared face. Johnny rushed over to stop this and help Alvar. Despite Guy's menace that was now focusing on Johnny as he helped Alvar up, Johnny was able to stop the beating. He made sure Alvar was able to walk. They left him to make it home alone. They meant to inflict physical punishment on Alvar for Guy's prior humiliation, but not fatal harm.

When Alvar had returned to an empty home, breathing labored, increasingly lightheaded, badly bruised and bleeding from the mouth, he didn't want to make a fuss. His mother was going to be really upset about this. Anyway, he knew his mother was in the middle of some intense work with Orcas that day, so he didn't call her. She was out on the boat anyway. Nor did he call a neighbor. Nor did he call an ambulance for himself. He felt defeated and ashamed and didn't want to rat on his attackers. After all, he had gotten the last good punch in, which likely broke Guy's nose. He wanted to sleep it off, he felt so tired, and figured he could face any music tomorrow. He had been through this before. It was like an initiation. If they persisted in bullying him after this, he would find each one alone, teach them a lesson individually, and then hopefully this would all be resolved. He went to straight to bed. He never woke up. Alvar died quietly and alone.

When she docked the boat late in the evening and noted her dark home in the short distance, Delora didn't think much of it. Alvar was likely asleep. Delora had just had the worse day ever out at sea with the Orcas, and she had witness Hototo's death only hours ago. She was emotionally and physically exhausted. She could only imagine the disruption the death would cause in the daily activity of the Orca family and wondered if she should even bother going out the next day. The thought of Alvar's sleeping head on his pillow made her smile. That was the only joy she felt all day. She was contemplating waking him up and telling him what happened, but decided that while it might help her to talk about it, he would be extremely upset and saddened at the news. She entered the house, quiet and alone, saw Alvar's coat thrown over the side of the couch and his shoes kicked off on the path to his room. She went right to bed.

**Orca: AKENEHI**

If Akenehi had not noted Hototo's problem with hearing recently, and his odd orientation earlier that morning, she would have been surprised at his blundered hunt. As she perceived him moving in too quickly towards the alert and threatening great white shark, she and the others shrieked out a warning at his error. Hototo either did not hear them or didn't care to acknowledge the warnings.

Perhaps the careful approach was not exciting enough. Hototo might have preferred a faster tempo, to feel the squish, the pulsing gushes, and the sensational rush of energy as the shark fought for its life. Whatever the reason, Hototo suddenly turned toward the shark approaching and in a burst of speed went in for the kill—massive chomps in quick succession that, in theory, would sever his great prey in two—then release the quick blinding cloud of delicious fluid he craved. In his youthful bloodlust Hototo had miscalculated. The shark was mortally and grotesquely wounded, but enough life and instinct remained that the meal had turned in a great predatory yet dying frenzy and tore massive, deep, jagged chunks of flesh from Hototo.

Akenehi rushed into the blood cloud while echolocating and vocalizing frantically. She knew much of the blood in the water was not shark but of her own kind, of her son, and that day, very soon, he would be lost to the deep, dark abyss to dissipate into the vastness that was the world she swam in. Hototo quickly returned to the air among his own screams and those of his family. He remained at the surface as his breathing was now shallow and labored. He had witnessed death in the family so he knew what was coming. Nonetheless, he became quiet, as did they all, as the screams and blood would likely have alerted other sharks nearby.

Akenehi, in brutal hindsight, realized she should have physically intervened as he approached his prey too quickly and from the wrong angle. She had failed to properly instruct her cherished Hototo and now the ocean would soon reclaim him. She had no desire to surrender any more of her beloved family to the ocean today. She calculated the time remaining before a shark feeding frenzy would likely develop. Food had been scarce and fatigue was taking its toll on all of them. Chaos had initially commanded them all, but Akenehi was already in the act of gathering their focus. They needed to remove Hototo from the area with the highest concentration of blood. She rose to the surface, inhaled deeply, and then emitted the unmistakable commanding vocalization and tail slap of the matriarch summoning the attention of all within the sound of her.

Hototo was still alive, knowing he must not struggle. He knew he must allow himself to be pressed and supported by others to breathe until he could no longer do so.

Akenehi, assisted by Hototo's closest siblings, remained flanking him, stroking and vocalizing, taking turns lifting him for air. Others echo-scanned the water for any pursuing sharks. There were none so far, and most of the bleeding was contained as his siblings took turns pressing firmly against the gashes to control the flow. Hototo managed to remain silent for the most part, as he was no longer feeling much pain and was losing the struggle to continue under his own power. Mercifully, he did not have to suffer a long death, as he had witnessed in others. That day he would breathe his last.

In the long moments leading up to that last breath, Hototo recalled the songs of his family and especially his favorite, the story of how Orca-kind came to be. What must it have been like, he pondered, to have been one of those ancient singers, one of the greatest chorus of all of Orca-kind, those who sang songs with such perfection and power that the very size and shape of their bodies were suddenly and permanently altered, made glorious and beautiful, more in the image of the One Mother. He recalled the songs his own grandmother had carefully taught him, meticulously handed down from grandmother to grandchild for countless generations. The history of his family—how, before any of them could remember, they used to be small and stupid, like the dolphins, but a wise and all-knowing grandmother had taught her clan a song so perfect and sang so worthy, our One Mother sought to make them one of her own and transformed them into the Orca-kind.

He sang one last song of love to his family and to his mother, Akenehi. He felt his energy fade as he listened to their own songs of love for him in return and wondered how long it would be before his body would be taken by the sea completely, consumed until only his bones remained and that flesh re-consumed until he at last came to be among his family again.

They had been swimming out to one of a few select places where so many had been released before. As it became obvious to all of them he was taking his last breath, they sang their good-bye and sorrow and then they joined in the chorus of his name. As was customary, they then all fell silent and listened for his heartbeat. Hototo shuddered, vocalized weakly, and then his strong young heart stopped altogether. His family, in formation, touched him and each other and waited for Akenehi's signal that he had passed the threshold of Orca life and was ready for release. She was completely exhausted with grief and physical effort. She could scarcely support a jellyfish, let alone their beloved Hototo. She softly sang her signal indicating it was time. All that was left was for the clan to accompany his sinking body as far down as the pressure could be tolerated then return in unison for a collective breath. The family had of course experienced death before, and each knew at the end of life all bodies would sink, to never rise for air again. The collective rise for breath was a ritual affirmation that for them life went on.

The life of an Orca was one of intimacy with nature, with the cycle of life and of death, the power of the ocean and the oneness that all life belonged to, came from, returned to and somehow found its way back out again. And with all this was their music, which told of their history, uniqueness and harmony with their world. The rest of the night was spent singing and grieving and reviewing the events that led up to this disaster. All of this brought Akenehi little comfort. Suffering was part of the Orca being, she mused. Her beloved Hototo was to be gone from her side from this day forward. She recalled his birth, that warm red cloud from which her infant emerged, the first breath at the surface which she assisted him in and beheld in anxiety and tenderness. She would no longer stroke the length of his body with her pectoral fin as they lazily napped near the surface. He would no longer break the surface water with his growing dorsal fin, which, had he survived might have been the tallest to be seen among the pod in generations.

The family continued to sing and grieve, and all, especially Akenehi, knew despite their current anguish and loss, there would be an echo of him throughout their lives and in a very real sense Hototo's strong, young, beautiful song would have no end.

**Sperm Whale: BROUGH**

Brough, at 52 years old, was a 48-ton sperm whale by human terms, a Long Jaw by Orca terms, and Master of the Ocean by his own species' terms. He was born into a family of 12 Masters including his many mothers and their children, beloved to him as brothers and sisters no matter the actual genetic relation. As was normal for his species, all females shared their milk and parenting between each other's calves with lifelong attachments. The result of this upbringing was that the entire pod was a close-knit and devoted family. He grew up in their communal love and protection, knowing each pod member almost as well he knew himself. To be a Master of the Ocean meant taking comprehensive and continual canvases of themselves, each other and their world. Their journeys started at birth, under the constant guidance and company of the close family unit.

Although they had superior memory and shared collective knowledge, they highly prized the uniqueness of each individual. Masters of the Ocean appreciated the value of the solitary journey, which spread their numbers over long distances and ensured prey was not overhunted. Equally as important, solitude forced deep reflection and interpretation of daily events. He had begun his first solo adventure, as was common for males his kind, during his 11th year.

On their way to nowhere in particular and everywhere possible, Masters of the Ocean visited and sometimes lived for years with other pods. Masters considered themselves one large extended family, even though for much of their lives they lived away from their original mother group. During this privileged lifetime, one would amass and communicate to other Masters data-rich clicks of information cataloguing the multitude of living beings, availability and size of prey, detailed fluid dynamics, changing landscapes of the ocean floor and the familiar and foreign bodies that found rest and recycling there. They also shared exciting details of their adventures defending against their only two predators: Orcas and humans. The stories and memories of each click were processed and valued. The ocean was truly never the same place twice and the Masters knew its lessons and mysteries best.

When it came to raw intelligence and mental processing, no other living being on the planet even came close. To be a Master of the Ocean was to be beyond words and whistles. Their echolocation skills replaced any language or song-based communication. While other cetaceans echolocated in combination with whistles, nothing compared to the Masters' absolute superiority in this natural ability. They processed and conveyed whole, comprehensive landscapes, both within and outside of their bodies. "How are you?" would be nonsensical to them. With one scan they knew gender, health, hunger, heart rate, injuries, and variations in density of bodies. They could "see" through the bottoms of boats, scanning content the same way. The images that were formed in their minds were not static in any sense of the word. Their brains processed environment, their own emotional and physical state and even the temperature and pressure of the ocean water simultaneously. They understood and knew and were aware as nothing else could possibly be. They were truly Masters of the Ocean.

The greatest purpose of all was to master awareness of the world's mysteries, infinite in scale. Their large brains and superior echolocation provided detail and mental processing of the returning data that revealed critical macro and microscopic information. The ocean was an infinite mystery in itself. Fulfilling a Master's nomadic life purpose entailed accumulating decades of experience, knowledge, and wisdom, which of course was also infinite in scale. Despite the collective knowledge that they all died, leaving mysteries unexamined, Brough was especially efficient and bold in his examination of anything of interest that returned in his echo. He loved the ocean dearly and wanted to know it all.

Brough was in his third decade of ocean survey, during which time he'd achieved an ability to detect certain extremely miniscule "bits" in the environment. If he had been able to discuss his perceptions with a human scientist he would have been told he detected microscopic details. This was relatively rare, but not unheard of in his species. The distinction of having the sensitivity to make these detections was a recognized life achievement and a prized ability. At any given time there were several of these "Aware" Masters scattered throughout the ocean, adding noteworthy microscopic observations to the collective knowledge base.

His journey included extended visits to his home pod. The first joyful reunion was during his 20$^{th}$ year. During that happiest of times he, along with other visiting males, protected and fed the new mothers as they nursed the calves, a most vulnerable period. They shared long conversations of their vast travels through clicks full of data and emotion. The young gathered information from these clicks as if they had been traveling themselves.

It was during this time one of the mothers and her new calf explored too far, just past the outer range of the newborn safety zone, and were heading back when they were located and pursued by Orcas, their most common and feared enemy. Several of the males immediately mobilized toward the sound of the Orcas, knowing by their hunting calls there was imminent danger to the infant. The Masters followed the booming successive bursts of frantic echolocation fired off by the mother as she deftly defended her child and summoned assistance in fending off the attack.

Brough knew firsthand the savagery these monsters could inflict on an infant. When he was a very young Master himself, he had heard the distinctive Orca hunting calls and viewed the result of their success—a mortally wounded infant. Large sections of its body had been stripped of its skin and underlying fatty layer, before being left alive with his injured and despairing mother. She and the rest of the pod attempted to keep it breathing at the surface. All watched the scene in horror and helplessness as the baby died in anguish.

He would sooner be skinned alive himself than have this happen to one of his beloved family, especially to an infant. Fortunately, help arrived in time and the Orcas were forced away from the child. The perimeter was patrolled heavily soon after, with frequent echolocation bursts that reassured all and gave knowledge to other distant pods of their success against the attack and the current safety of all.

Now at 52 years old, those memories came back in force and clarity when, during his next casual sonar burst, Brough detected an Orca pod about two miles away. He gave a 360 degree radar scan and quickly determined they were the only pod within a ten mile radius. They were heading in his general direction now but he felt no fear. As a full-grown adult, he had a sure-fire defense against Orca. Aside from sheer size and strength, he would simply dive below their limit, an easily obtainable 300 meters. If necessary he could continue down for another 1,900 meters assuring his safety as, unlike a Master, Orcas were not able to survive the pressure.

Any fear he felt would have been for vulnerable members of his own kind in the area. However, his scan revealed the Orcas had a seriously injured member and they were most definitely not on the hunt. He gave a succession of bursts that would alert any Masters within a very large distance the location and number of these beasts before he very calmly made preparation for a deep dive.

He remained in the area, scanning and observing the Orca pod's approach, their pause and descent to their own limited depths. He had moved almost directly under the pod as they descended and was intensely interested in what was occurring. He had never directly scanned such a ritual but he had received information from other Masters who had seen similar. He felt extremely fortunate he had happened to be surveying and hunting in their vicinity tonight.

The living Orcas turned and re-surfaced.

Brough was then the lone cetacean who observed with full sentience the just-dead corpse of the young male Orca as it continued sinking. In total darkness, pressure and cold, he scanned the massive, still-whole Orca, a body silent and full of potential energy. He noted the unmistakable injury from the Great White, contemplating the boldness of his enemy to undertake such a challenge. He swam close enough to feel the dissipating but still present heat energy that would eventually be transferred completely to the surrounding waters.

He turned downward and scanned the ocean floor. The corpse was on a course to land directly in a tangled insult of human debris and netting.

This would not do.

He intensified his clicks and found an adjacent unlittered area. Brough positioned himself under Hototo's body and guided it gently to that place.

He did this for several reasons. Obviously, all Masters were caretakers of the ocean and they did such things out of natural duty. It was a matter of safety for the organisms who would feed on the remains. The human netting was littered with the bodies of hapless creatures that had become entangled and died while simply recycling the biomatter within the debris field. Far better the Orca was placed where the living ocean preferred. Further, he felt it was extremely distasteful for any creature, even a natural enemy, to land in such a nonsensical configuration.

A swirling cloud of bioluminescence and soft organic debris danced around the Orca as his weight displaced matter on the seabed. Brough rose above it then turned downward to scan the multitude of living organisms within that cloud and surrounding area. Several fish of varying types were already beginning to consume the body now that the Orcas were not able to protect it. He marveled at the returning echoes detailing the intricate excited swirls of movement. Their complex formations around the flesh that would soon be recycled in other organisms were a privilege to observe.

Brough reflected deeply on the peace of the current surroundings, its hidden complex beauty and dynamics and the world's common sense of a single life's cycle.

He moved to the jumble of netting and scanned the puzzle. Some entrapped fish were still alive and struggling. After careful analysis, ensuring he himself would not be injured or become entangled, he was able to achieve release for some with careful manipulation of the heap. He did not eat them. He simply released them because it was the right thing to do. He took careful note of the location, size and contents of the rubbish pile and eventually moved away in search of giant squid.

## CHAPTER TWO: DAY TWO

### Human: DELORA

When Delora woke up she went to the kitchen and started coffee as usual, then called for Alvar to wake up for school. When he didn't respond, she didn't react. Still very distraught over the previous day's events, she was intensely contemplative and not responsive to the outside world. Then she noticed it was getting late. Alvar would be tardy if he didn't get up now. She went into his room and stood over him, looking more at the familiar chaotic mess of his room rather than directly at him.

Then she turned her eyes to Alvar and waited for him to stir. To her horror he had obviously been beaten. She saw his blood. He remained still, eyes fixed and opened. Delora froze in disbelief for a moment and took in the whole scene, following her child's empty gaze to see what he might have been looking at. It appeared to be the only object on his nightstand, a model of a spherical carbon-60 molecule he had constructed. She must still be dreaming, she thought, a nightmare as a result of Akenehi's horrific loss of Hototo. But Delora dissolved into panic as she realized she was indeed awake.

Disoriented and desperate, she tried to call for help, grasped for her phone but found her fingers wouldn't work. She fumbled with it and it tumbled out of her hands and onto Alvar's body. Delora let out a gasp and reached down to soothe him. She held her next breath and listened and waited. He didn't flinch when the phone hit him. He did not respond to her touch. The whole house was too quiet. It was unnatural. She carefully reached down and took his pulse at the neck. Nothing.

Her initial generalized panic transformed. She calculated furiously. The person or persons who had done this might still be in the house, their home. The safety bubble their home enclosed them in had burst. The wild was not limited to the outside of the structure, kept at bay to the woods or sea. The wild was within those walls as well; predator and prey. Danger. *Death.*

Only, the danger she perceived was not for *her*. The mere suggestion that she was at risk of being injured or worse would have been nonsensical. She felt the surging turbulence of her blood delivering news of arrival. A capable predator was within her and she surfaced with lethal intent. She sought to *kill* someone. The wild was in her, unleashing an ancient and powerful maternal rage. Whoever did this to her son, if they were clumsy enough to remain in her proximity at that moment, was about to die. She took inventory of Alvar's body, the room and considered possibilities. She moved quickly and lightly to collect various items to use as distractors and weapons. She envied Akenehi more than she ever had. Damn those objects; she wanted nothing more than to sever her prey in one mighty chomp. She waited for any sound of approaching or retreating footsteps, within or outside of the house. Everything was quiet.

She crouched low, every muscle fully powered and ready to spring, carefully moving to avoid any spot that might creak under her feet. The house was small enough to cover quickly. Soon she determined there was no intruder. Her prey had eluded her, for now.

She returned to where her son lay. Alvar had taught her to look beyond her own human senses and ability. Universes full of free choice, possibility, and alternative outcomes would open if one had the right key. If she agreed he was dead and began acting as if he was, she would set off a chain of events that would make it so. There was hope for Alvar but she would have to take action. Without a guide or precedent what could she possibly do? Could anyone help her?

She remembered Alvar himself had actually offered to help her with such a situation. She began to recover her senses. The memory of his voice was clear and instructive.

*"You look sad. What's the matter?"*

*They were heading back to land after a day on the water. He knew plainly what was bothering her but he was just starting the conversation. One of the Orca pods, not Akenehi's, had suffered a loss of one of their young. Infant mortality was high among the pods but that didn't make it less painful.*

*"Oh, I was just thinking. I don't know what I would do if something happened to you, you know if..."*

*Alvar tried to reassure her. "Nothing is going to happen to me, Mom." He grinned. "Don't worry. Anyway, if the worst happens just go back in time and change it. Undo it. Bring me back!"*

*"And just how would I do that? I think I'd just have to join you. It would be too sad to go on without you."*

*With that Alvar became serious. "No. What would you want me to do if I lost you? Just go and kill myself? No! I'll help you thought it. I'll be there, don't worry." Then he lightened the mood once more. "Anyway if time travel doesn't work you can have another kid and then I can haunt him. I always wanted a little brother to torment."*

*She rolled her eyes away from him and looked out over the water. She didn't answer and he saw she remained quiet and sullen. He tried another tactic.*

*"Okay, let's say I died. Assuming it's not from some incurable disease, a car accident. Put your emotions aside and think. Don't think about stuff like the gross way my body might look. Think about time traveling back to save me. When you time travel back the crash can be prevented. Okay, what do you do next?"*

*"Alvar, if people could time travel everyone would be doing it. Nothing bad would ever happen and no mother would ever lose her child."*

*"Come on, we have to figure this out! Remember all those paradoxes I told you about? We have to work this out. What do you do next?"*

*"Well, apparently I'll have to accept your offer and wait for you to help me, because I will have absolutely* no idea *how to proceed."*

*"Okay, be on the lookout then."*

*When his mother let out a doubtful 'Pffff.' he became annoyed.*

*"I mean it, Mom. Pay attention!"*

The conversation had turned to something else, fading away into obscurity. But now, she looked around carefully. She studied the carbon-60 molecule model—a soccer ball shape of twenty hexagons and twelve pentagons on his nightstand. He had been looking at it to the very end.

She considered what his last thoughts might have been during those moments. Had he experienced much pain? Had he wanted her near him? Did he know he was dying?

Alvar always told her he believed her concept of death was oversimplified and limited. Delora had told him of her knowledge that death happened in stages. While brain death was certainly an early and decisive event, certain cells in the body continued to live on for a few hours after brain death, functions remained capable, if not active, for a time. A heart could be kept beating, a brain cell could be stimulated with an electrode and the body would react. But once *all* functions ceased, Delora believed the body was truly dead and life as she defined it was permanently and irretrievably lost.

Alvar had emphatically disagreed. He could not accept an abyss or permanent ending. It was counterintuitive and defied logic. Energy was the essence of life, not biology, and once passed on it would manifest any abilities dependent on configuration and context. The universe to Alvar's mind was alive and it wanted life. Everywhere it *could* be alive, in any form, it *would* be. He pointed to the existence of carbon 60 molecules in deep space. There it was, evidence of the universe's omnipresent life force, waiting for its chance to develop and thrive. In that way Alvar understood energy was one living entity, flowing fluid or passing in concentrated masses from location to location. He believed he could never truly die as his entire being was energy in one form or another He had won her over then and she held fast to his words.

She remembered he told her specifically to put her emotions aside. It was nearly impossible. Alvar's fixed gaze reminded her of his focus.

Alvar had called it a C-cage for short, and the name had stuck. She had bought him the tools and materials as a gift to show support for his ideas. She had been intrigued when he explained why he had taken such meticulous care to construct his C-cage. This was a model of an actual molecule, but the molecule itself, as Alvar had energetically exclaimed to her, "…is relatively common and found in soot and has even been detected in deep space. It has a carbon atom at each vertex. And it exhibits wave properties! Maybe it has something to do with genetic mutations..."

During their long days out at sea Alvar had explained the theories of quantum biology and spontaneous mutation of genes, the dual nature (wave and particle) of light, energy, and certain organic molecules, time travel and multiple universes that he found most intriguing. Alvar speculated that through this specific carbon-60 arrangement perhaps miniscule undetectable quantum events could actually be captured and expanded to a scale we could actually observe, manipulate, and possibly even time travel and conduct visits to alternate multiple universes.

Hadn't he eventually succeeded in convincing her time travel was not only possible, but they might even do it some day? He imaged time travel obstacles and paradoxes would be overcome if other universes with the correct features could be utilized. He was sure limits of his universe need not apply to the entire multiverse. It seemed reasonable, in theory; time travel could be accomplished by a combination of temporal merging and a variation of a multiple universe solution to avoid a temporal paradox. Yes, Delora agreed with Alvar. Time travel to the past might seem highly *improbable* but not *impossible* however.

She also recalled the day Alvar had taken the model, as part of a research trial, out to the Orcas. Inventing a simple human/Orca vocabulary of nouns was one of her research projects. Delora and Alvar had many unique opportunities to learn to communicate with them. Alvar had presented a few novel human-made objects he found most interesting in order to record "inquisitive" Orca vocalizations. Orcas were rarely really interested in human objects. It was the humans themselves that interested them. Holding any cetacean's attention was very challenging. Nonetheless, Alvar placed the spherical metal model in the basketball-sized net attached to Delora's long extendable pole apparatus and presented it to the cetaceans for examination. Responses, if any, would be observed and vocalizations recorded.

Akenehi had shown an immediate and noticeable interest in his molecule model and the Orcas took turns approaching it. Delora had recorded a cacophony of extraordinary vocalizations that day and had been very pleased with Alvar's inspiration. When the Orcas interacted with the C-cage in close range many of the vocalizations dropped in wavelength, sounding very similar to notes that might be played on a cello rather than their usual scratchy violin sounds.

Unfortunately Alvar lost control of the net upon retrieval and the model was lost to the ocean—at least, they had both assumed it was lost. Akenehi had surprised Alvar by flipping it up out of the water to him. Delora had certainly observed new behavior and cooperation between humans and Orcas that day. She was glad it had been returned, though. Not only was it the fruit of Alvar's labor to meticulously construct it, but it was now an object that served as a physical connection to this very happy memory that she and Alvar shared.

Delora started to connect dots. Those past events were not random. They were progressions toward discovery. Akenehi and her son had opened up an eternity of possibilities beyond human perception and comprehension. She taught him to look beyond his species and he taught her to look beyond her own life and universe. If solutions existed to this problem – and she was in problem solving mode – they were clearly beyond her human ability.

Who could help her? Akenehi could, of course. Delora imagined she saw Alvar standing beside her, nodding in agreement. They had all been gravitating on instinct toward the place and time, like a spawning salmon, with purpose, but without a conscious thought of the end result. She was going to follow that instinct to its destination.

She stood and hooked the molecule model under her index finger and lifted it as one might pick up a set of keys on a large ring. It was a key, Alvar had said, and it was the help she needed. She placed her hand gingerly under it for support and turned back to Alvar. At that moment the view of his face appeared to her line of sight as positioned between the empty spaces of the model. Alvar looked as if he was in his C-cage. He'd made a coherent suggestion, a plan of action.

There was a story in him, and it was not ended. It was only days ago he said '*Energy never dies'*. His story was his energy. Delora accepted his point of view. Alvar's *death* had not occurred because his *energy* still existed. There was an opportunity for a do-over. She trusted Alvar completely. It was not too late.

Delora stiffened, replaced the model where she had found it, hastily left his room, grabbed her coat and her muddied shoes she used only for gardening and lawn work. She hurriedly slipped them on, feeling she had a train to meet and was running late, and went back in to Alvar, gave him one last kiss on the cheek, paused as she touched her forehead to his, then stood up. She almost forgot to take the C-cage with her. Model securely in hand; she admonished herself to stay sharp for possible signs on how to proceed.

*First, find Akenehi.* She purposefully headed out of the house without even pausing to lock up, and walking as quickly as she could without running, she went straight to her boat, started it up and sped out to open ocean. She kept going, like the Orcas swam with Hototo, looking for some sacred space, until she was finally satisfied she had gone far enough. She felt peace and order and it helped her resolve. She took one last look back, in the direction of home, which was no longer visible.

Delora no longer associated land with belonging. Her perspective of her place in the world was shifting. Despite her excellent swimming skills, water had always been a floor to her, a chaotic membrane threatening to swallow her or her son up if she didn't take the proper precautions. Now it was land that was treacherous and fatal. That day, the ocean surface was soft and safe, even inviting. The gentle tossing of each wave reminded her of Alvar happily bouncing on her knee when he was a toddler. Their best moments had been right there on the boat, on the open sea and in that way she was carrying him away with her.

She cut off the engine suddenly, as if she had seen a huge stop sign. This area of the water looked the same as any other, but this was definitely the place, she thought. That feeling of following instructions, like the instinct of a salmon determined to force its way upriver, had not vanished.

With practiced skill, she turned on her equipment and through it generated the pre-recorded, usually successful summons to Akenehi and the pod. She had recorded the vocalizations of the Orcas during the shark incident yesterday. Now, she added those too, in hopes they would be an effective attractant rather than repellant; and elicit an immediate and urgent interest to examine the source of the replay. She amplified and repeated it, then cut it off and waited with the quiet splashing of water against the hull.

Finally she saw them approaching. She watched Akenehi's curved, and familiar notched fin come ever closer until the Orcas surrounded the boat. All exhaled in unison and produced a delicate mist into the cool air. It gave a familiar dream-like atmosphere to the encounter and Delora felt like they were confirming to her she was on the right path to another world.

She looked around for Hototo's distinctive tall dorsal fin, hoping she had been mistaken, that his injury had not been fatal. He was not there. It was true then; *both* on the same day. Delora felt the sickening memory of death and it brought her back from her reverie. She thought of how she might help Akenehi understand what she wanted at this moment—wasn't even sure exactly what she expected from the family, what their role might be, except she wanted to be with them. Alvar and Akenehi shared an understanding with her and she looked for their further instruction. It was time to find Alvar alive and swim off with them forever.

*Second, get in the water.* There was nothing on land for her. She started to remove her shoes. She stopped herself. *No, leave them on.* What did it matter? Still on auto-pilot, watching herself from far away, fighting her way up that impossible river current, she picked up the C-cage and grasped it tightly; ready to resist the shock of the cold. She slipped over the side into the water, shoes, coat, and all. She gasped at the icy stabbing cold, panicked and floundered, and then in reflex, she screamed. She had let go. The key Alvar had provided her was sinking.

She managed to push off a few strokes away from the boat and let herself go under. She saw nothing, no white patches contrasting starkly against black that would indicate an Orca swimming nearby. She was beginning to feel fear. And so deeply cold. She dove a shallow bit and reached her arms in futile circles searching for the C-cage, but of course, she realized, it had already sunk. It was made of metal, after all, and she hadn't thought to attach a line to it.

She burst to the surface and was alarmed that she didn't see any Orcas. She was absolutely certain they should have been there. She felt something very large brush by, but hadn't seen a single pod member underwater with her. In her panic and sudden drop in body temperature she became quickly disoriented. Sharks were also in the area and she had acted rashly and was splashing around. Maybe her recording in combination with her jumping into the water had startled the Orca's and they feared for the younger members of their pod and had taken them away. Maybe they didn't trust her as much as Delora had hoped they did. Maybe they had disappeared and were very far away from her now. With her clumsy ruckus and floundering, surely every shark within a mile knew right where to find her.

Still no Orca in sight, she felt another brush. She clamped her eyes shut. She clenched her numbing body as tight as she could, in anticipation of a sudden violent death. Mercifully, she felt no pain other than cold. *Here we go, goddammit,* she thought to herself, assuming the brushes were test strikes from a shark.

As a scientist she believed in repeatable processes that produce predictable results. But her belief in whatever led her to *this* conviction was an instinctive emotional drive and not based on any linear methodology she had tested. Her inexperience with death might have left her vulnerable to knee-jerk emotional panic and nonsensical behavior. Time travel, of all things! Nonetheless, she wanted it to happen, hoped somehow it would work. She imagined Alvar urging her on, she only needed the courage, the reason, the resolve. She could will herself to time travel if she focused hard enough.

*Third….*

Then it hit her—white noise, warmth, singing, pressure…a hurricane seemed to rage within and around, vibrations like a jackhammer, a turbo stream of multiple experiences in a span of no time at all. Was this what it felt like to be brutally eaten alive? Without finding it strange in any way, she saw Alvar was near her, watching.

*She was back at home, in the past, warm, coffee in hand, and there he was. They were having* the talk.

*"Well," began Delora, "when I was only a few years older than you are now, I was arrested".*

*Delora anticipated that he would be shocked. She had always tried to be the perfect example of a human being. Aside from swearing, she had few vices, thought herself a wonderful parent, treated people with respect and obeyed the law. Hell, she had never even smoked so much as a cigarette, let alone something that might be illegal.*

*"What, for smoking..." he raised his eyebrows up and down in comical succession, "*weed?"

*Delora laughed. "Well, that was practically a requirement for graduation, you know. But that's not why I was arrested. No, I tried to get arrested, and I was proud of it. Stupid, huh?"*

*"Mom!" Alvar's smile was a big as Delora had ever seen it. She loved her son's smile. She lived for that smile. Her goal in life was to enjoy every moment of it and to be happy. Why had that been so difficult before Alvar? Now it came so frequently and naturally with him.*

*Delora leaned toward him, slowly looked over his face, and brushed his long, dark bangs away from his eyes. She drew in a slow breath then sighed. "You know I love you more than my own life. You're everything to me"*

"Mom*! Arrested! You said you were arrested!"*

*"Okay, okay. You know I've had a passion for cetaceans for as long as I can remember." Delora stood up and started slowly moving around the room, keeping her gaze mostly on Alvar, but looking out the window and looking deeply into her past. "Well, I wasn't sure what I wanted to do after I graduated college but I knew I wanted to 'Save the Dolphins! Save the Whales! Save the World! Change the World!' Anyway, to make a long story short, I went overseas and got involved with some anti-whaling demonstrations, but what you don't know is one got particularly ugly and I was arrested. I spent a couple of days in jail. My dear parents, by the way, refused to help or bail me out, and if it weren't for Grammy I probably would have*

*been there for a while."*

*"You never told me about the jail part. Cool! What did you do? Exactly. Tell me!"*

*"Oh, just...I was young and angry and no one was going to stop me and I wouldn't do what I was told by someone who had the power to stop me and well...I ended up in jail.*

*Delora's mind drifted and she was looking at Alvar's father in her mind's eye, remembering the exuberance of her arrest along with the few new passionate friends she had made; the final look at the only true love she had ever felt before Alvar.*

*"So... What happened in jail? What was it like?"*

*"Not much, and not good." She smiled at him. She recalled vividly the claustrophobic, helpless feeling of that short but traumatic confinement. Unfortunately, it had frightened her into compliance, into doing whatever she was told, to give up her fight against injustice. She would have done anything to get out of that cell. But the shame of those feelings was not to be shared with Alvar. "You know your father and I lost touch, and I never told you how. Well, now I'm telling you. We were arrested, separated and by the time I got out of jail I had to return home. That was a consequence of my actions. I lost contact with him. I was young and stupid and impulsive. And it ultimately cost you a relationship with your father."*

*Alvar quizzed her on why she slept with a guy she really didn't know. His question led directly to discussion on types of bonds people share, the concept of predestination, and then onto the subject of time travel. Delora had simply felt a very familiar bond with his father, instinctive, positive and powerful. She hypothesized that familiarity may well have been Alvar's presence in her future life beckoning her toward his existence.*

*They continued talking for hours. They laughed, shared fresh ideas on life and love and re-told stories they had shared many times before. They talked about the possibility that Alvar might be able to find him. Alvar, to her surprise, was not terribly interested in pursuing it, but Delora suspected he would change his mind, eventually.*

*Alvar was growing up and now they spoke as friends, not just mother and son. That was one of the best conversations they ever shared. Alvar forgave her. He wasn't angry at her as she imagined he would be when he knew the truth. She felt lighter about things that at the time were definitely not. Alvar had saved her from loneliness. He was the only happy family she had known. He made her own unhappy childhood acceptable as it was the only path to him.*

Drifting in the water, Delora visited other memories.

*The day she received the news that she was pregnant, she was initially terrified, because her long held future of a single, successful cetacean biologist was dead, and a new uncertain one was taking its place. She feared she would be a horrible parent. With the encouragement and support of her grandmother she found her feet again. Those fears vanished when she actually saw Alvar's precious little newborn face. Delora found she was silly in doubting herself when it came to motherhood. It took no work at all to love Alvar with all her being. The first time she held him, alone, late at night, still in the hospital, she cried so many tears of joy at holding him in her arms that her chin dripped with them, her neck was wet and the front of her nightgown was soaked. She never imagined her child could be so precious, so beautiful, so worth living for.*

*The memories started to dim. The conversations quieted until all that remained was the vivid aroma of the fresh skin of her newborn infant, its unbelievable softness and beauty, and her own sweet breast milk as she held him and nursed him for the first time. Being in that perfectly happy place, she relaxed completely and felt an acceptance and peace regarding her own end that until that moment could never have been achieved.*

Delora hit the floor of the boat with a squelching thud.

She awoke gasping, shivering, and gagging as she pulled herself onto the bench and grasped the rail as best she could. She forced herself silent as soon as she could, searching for shark fins in the water. She imagined a Great White had, most likely in error, bumped her clear back to safety instead of testing the tastiness of her flesh. She saw dorsal fin break water and felt panic.

No. Wait…

Not a shark. She *knew* that dorsal fin. The large black curve of the fin identified it as Akenehi. She saw other fins as they retreated. She knew them all. They had not swum away but instead saved her, prevented her drowning. She looked out over the water and saw Akenehi and the pod surfacing as they departed.

Her pristine recall of the entire torrent of memory that had just pulled her in amazed her. The experience was not fading as time progressed. Even intense memories fade in many details, but not these. What at the time was perceived at white noise had actual identifiable parts. It was like she had been granted admittance to an ocean library and could read its volumes like three dimensional books in her mind. She hoped she would be able to hold on to these experiences with unfading clarity. They had changed her.

From across the water she heard the Orcas singing. Emotion swelled up in her and she had no words. She sat up and called out to the retreating pod she could not join. She was shivering, alone, wondering what would become of her life without Alvar. Delora decided that she must have time traveled, and for some reason Akenehi had brought her back. She thought for a moment about jumping back in for another try, but it was no good. Animal survival was taking over. She was too cold and too emotional. But returning to a normal human life was not going to happen either. If human nature claimed her completely, she would give up her journey toward time travel, would lose the courage to take the associated risks, put herself in danger, defy common sense. She could not allow her own human life to become such a focus and distraction that she abandoned Alvar's work. She knew she would have to fight for its continuance from that moment until a natural death claimed her. She longed to be physically Orca and swim away with Akenehi and her clan, but it could not be. Not yet. However, the white noise memories she was left with were not human. Delora was satisfied with that compromise.

Over the water, toward dry land, where her old life had been, and where her remaining human life must continue, she saw an approaching light. A boat was heading right toward her that carried at least one other human soul. She wondered who it would be. No one close to her remained. It could not possibly be Alvar. Could it? For a moment she believed it was.

She had been mistaken and merely in a deep sleep, he had awoken, he had come looking for her and had found her. The Orcas had responded and helped her. She looked down on the boat floor and saw the C-cage. Akenehi or one of the other Orcas had retrieved it and had given it back to her. For the first time that day she felt it might not be so bad if she had to stick around a while longer.

**Orca: AKENEHI**

Akenehi and the clan were still in the area, still grieving, unwilling to leave Hototo's remains too far behind for the time being. They were in stealth mode as they were on the hunt for a large prey item. They listened quietly for its massive heartbeat, any echo clicks it might give away, its intestinal sounds, and the like. They'd heard Delora's familiar engine in the distance but were all taken completely by surprise when they heard the loud, rude replay of yesterday's awful events. The recording was unnatural sounding and none of them thought for a moment it was actually Hototo, as they clearly recognized the pathetically poor acoustic qualities of Delora's playbacks. But something was wrong, Akenehi was sure of it.

They all had plenty of experience with this particular boat and the *land squid* that accompanied it. This is what Akenehi and her clan called humans. She had heard her grandmother use this description and also recognized in them the many appendages and the squid-like grappling and flailing behaviors. Land squid were much more unpredictably dangerous than those of the ocean. Akenehi had witnessed more than one surprisingly cunning hunt where Orcas were uncharacteristically the prey. Long ago, land squid had removed her daughter forever from their ocean. Other Orca clans had reported land squid injured or killed some of their family.

But not these particular land squid. These were benign, unusually interesting and even somewhat dear to them. Akenehi was most attached to them, especially the younger, obviously mutated male who never failed to amuse. She had suspected he was the offspring of the female due to the Orca-like maternal protection and instruction she obviously exhibited.

These sounds were out of the ordinary and very bizarre but more urgently, they were likely alerting their prey. The recording pulled them off the hunt for the moment to investigate. As they approached the boat they recognized as Delora's, they formed a circle and continued intensified echo-scanning. They were all startled when Delora suddenly jumped into the water. Their returning echoes informed them she had unusual loose fitting materials around her and possessed that intriguing object again. When Delora involuntarily dropped it, a younger member of the family positioned lower than the others successfully darted down, capturing it before it sank beyond their jaws. He held it in his mouth for only a moment and then members of his clan took turns taking it, passing it back and forth, dropping it from above to another directly below. They were perfecting their memory and reproduction of the dynamic and beautiful resonances that played around in and off of it.

The resulting tones were nothing short of amazing. Urgent and intense effort was expended by all to commit this powerful new song to memory. All practiced in quick succession, taking great pride in their skill at replicating fascinating delicate nuances. Again, they rolled and swayed rhythmically, expressing sheer joy with the dance of their sleek graceful bodies. The water displacement caused by their dance was creating its own pleasant tactile sensations. If not for their grievous loss of the day before, this would have been one the best spontaneously happy events the clan had ever known. There were familiar qualities reverberating through the water that suggested the ancient refrains of how Orca-kind was created and favored above all beings. The ocean recognized the pattern and the water itself joined in the harmony and dance.

Then Akenehi stole the show. Her family fell silent and listened as she, using the object as a tuning instrument, perfected and improvised and almost transported them with her beautiful singing. Many of them expressed later that when listening to her they perceived themselves floating effortlessly and feeling more joy than they had in a very long time.

Akenehi soon noticed with deep concern that Delora was moving strangely even for an ungainly land squid. Rather than repeat her failure of yesterday where she ignored her instincts with catastrophic results, she paid close attention to Delora's heart rate and realized it was not right for her species. Akenehi knew she might have to intervene. She echo-scanned Delora intensely, and noted no illness or injury, but focused on her weak human hearing and vocal mechanisms. Akenehi hypothesized by pooling the new harmonics and resonance patterns with traditional healing songs she might enhance Delora's ability to hear and vocalize in a more Orca-like manner. Delora and her son had obviously been trying to teach the Orcas, but when the Orcas had tried to teach them in return, they seemed partially deaf and unresponsive.

Akenehi realized that any vocal enhancements would be useless to the clan unless Delora's hearing could be correspondingly improved. Tampering with ears gave her pause. This was where she had made a most unforgiveable mistake with her own son Hototo. Using their new harmonics they had tried to repair Hototo's hearing and balance only a short time before his accident. Obviously she had failed, though the clan would not let her accept blame for the calamity. Nevertheless, she would not risk damaging any others of her clan until these songs were perfected. However, using a land squid to test their ability seemed reasonable. Delora was not Orca-kind and the modifications would be appreciated and useful, Akenehi was certain.

Akenehi utilized her acoustic instruments and within mere moments, delicate physical modifications were shaped into Delora's vocal mechanisms and confirmed with an echo scan. An attempt was begun to enhance Delora's hearing, but it seemed to elicit a pain reaction and associated squid-flailing, so Akenehi ceased. She continued to observe and it became obvious that despite a lack of physical injury Delora was exhibiting unusual behavior.

Akenehi determined this unfortunate land squid was not able to return to the boat on her own. Akenehi came forward at the moment Delora began to go limp and lifted her as gently as she could, balancing the human weight up through the surface and back over the side of the boat. Akenehi was moved by her small frail body. She experienced a quite unexpected almost familial protective affection for this land squid. The clan observed Akenehi's tender rescue behavior and settled down.

Orcas did not usually have pets as humans did. Nonetheless, Delora was after that day Akenehi's pet, and she worried for her wellbeing. The land squid had possibly suffered very grievous recent loss. All mature Orcas easily recognized those distinct physiological indicators. Akenehi hoped Delora would recover from her grief with her modified voice and they might one day perfect their communication. Perhaps Akenehi could even teach Delora simple but useful Orca songs.

Perceiving the lesson was coming to an end, the clan quieted so a few of the older, wiser Orcas might perfect the curious hollow, open qualities associated uniquely with the object. Knowing they could not keep it and hunt, and it would eventually have to be dropped to the ocean floor, at Akenehi's direction, the young Orca flipped it deftly in the boat.

In earnest, they whistled and clicked the significance of this encounter. Akenehi hypothesized to the clan that Delora perhaps recognized the special acoustic qualities the object could elicit and knew Orcas could put that to use, and perhaps was offering it to them. Akenehi concluded the call today was a form of specific communication or statement of purpose on Delora's part, though the purpose was not indisputably clear. Akenehi suspected they might be presented with this object again. In any case, they all agreed Delora's appearance with the shape had definitely provided them with critical pieces of a tonal puzzle.

Concluding the interaction with Akenehi's special land squid, the clan sang one of their most powerful healing songs, one with calming and soothing meaning that would serve to ease their own fresh emotional wounds as well. They sang it out to her, adding improvised low frequency burping human sounds and newly perfected tones as they continued away from her boat until Akenehi gave the all quiet.

Their prior hunt had required stealth, and they returned to it. The clan had prey to pursue and energy to regain. They resumed searching in vain for the deep location of a long jaw heard echolocating in the immediate area prior to their arrival at Delora's boat but could no longer detect him. None faulted Delora's interference for the failed hunt, as their own vocalizations and movement surely tipped anything in the area off. It had been a risky hunt as it sounded like a large male, and normally that would have saved him from pursuit. Their hunger was growing intensely powerful and with one less hunter in the family, life was not getting easier for any of them.

**Sperm Whale: BROUGH**

Brough sent powerful volleys of echo bursts toward the stationary boat and the encircling Orcas. When the Human entered the water Brough was surprised; then alarmed at the subsequent reaction of the Orcas to a familiar shaped human object. He had received clicks from other Master's throughout his life containing details of the fearsome intelligence Orcas exhibited, but this was completely unprecedented.

He was baffled by the compassion the lead female showed to the human female when she returned her back to the boat. Had he misunderstood their hunting behavior toward him? His scans confirmed that the Orca stomachs were quite empty. No, they had definitely been hunting him just moments prior, but there was something non-predatory and even unique about this human/Orca interaction. Both species were natural enemies to Masters, countless centuries of murder towards his kind. This resembled cooperation and possibly worse. The object the Orcas were examining sent shudders of elevated awareness through his body.

At the risk of alerting the Orcas to his exact location, which was almost right under them, he strengthened his echoes so the return contained as much detail of this singular scene as possible. At those powerful bursts several fish that just happened to be swimming by in front of him instantly died, stunned and killed by his blasts. Brough was too intently focused to examine the damage his blasts had on those fish and let them sink, unnoticed.

He noted the human had carried at least one sacred bit very close to her body at the end of one of her appendages. A human scientist that studied this sacred bit would have called it a spherical fullerene carbon-60 molecule. Brough wondered if either the human or the Orcas could possibly be aware of it, as he believed only his kind could be cognizant that it was even present. He was in disbelief that the smaller brained creatures would be able to share his fine perception. No, he did not wish to believe a bit was intentionally placed there. No doubt, he consoled himself, the larger sacred-bit self-similar object she released and the Orca's had returned to her were known to all of them. There was also no doubt—confirmed by his echo—in Brough's mind that the shapes were the same, even though they were of incredibly different scales. He had never imagined he would encounter a bit shape so large that even an Orca would be aware of it. That worried him greatly. He would have liked to repeat bursts with varying angles and sequences over more time, but he was the object of a most dangerous, albeit brazen and unlikely to be successful, Orca hunt. Death was not a threat; however he did not wish injury. He could not linger.

He would seek out Param, the most knowledgeable Aware he knew of, and consult with her about what this could mean. She was much older than he, and there was no guarantee she was still alive. The ocean was large and he did not know exactly where she had last been or how long it would take to come within communication range of a Master who did know her location, but the process of finding her needed to begin immediately. He pushed off with a powerful down-up-and-down stroke of his lower body, and continued echolocation scans as he went. He sent off his first signature call that identified himself and carried the request to locate her specifically.

Hours passed as he rose for breath, dove, hunted, ate and contemplated. He processed the day's events. What worried him the most, what he could not fathom, was the interaction between the human, the Orcas and the large sacred-shaped object. It was one of the most riveting and meaningful scenes he had ever scanned his whole life. He had eluded the Orcas easily and began his journey to Param, but he could not dive deep enough to escape his memory of the events. As all Masters know, the ocean carried memories, some of them were Param's own, and he browsed, as was customary for his kind, as he went. He had added his experience to its volumes and sent its message out to all Masters. He searched the ocean's subtle whispers for anything that she might have left that would calm his mind until he found her.

## CHAPTER THREE: DURING THE NEXT SIX MONTHS

### Human: DELORA

The boat pulled up.

Of course it couldn't be Alvar and it wasn't. It was the Coast Guard. Two men, locals, who called her by name.

What had happened was this—Alvar had indeed broken Guy's nose, and this injury required a trip to the hospital. Guy had not been willing to divulge the details of the incident, but one of the other three, Johnny, had fessed up. Johnny had been very concerned about the brutality of the attack and was worried about Alvar. He himself had been severely beaten by his father, the town's most notorious alcoholic, and that beating had almost killed him. No amount of teenage rivalry or jealousy could make him wish that on anyone. Johnny did not want to face Alvar at school, so he confided in his mother in the morning. She immediately called the police. Johnny had been in trouble with the law before this incident, and Johnny's mother was anxious to make sure Alvar was all right.

When the police finally came around to check on Alvar, they saw Delora as she left in the boat. They had called after her, but the engine was already engaged. She did not perceive them or turn around. The door was unlocked as they entered and then they discovered Alvar, as Delora had, cold and still. They became immediately concerned about Delora's mental state and called the Coast Guard to go after her.

Theirs was a small town, and not much ever happened of real consequence, so the death of Alvar traumatized not only the young men who had a hand in his death, but the whole community. The village stood still for the days immediately following the tragedy. Delora spent the first day at the hospital, but because she was found inside the boat and not floating outside of it, she wasn't held on suicide watch and was released. Her doctor nonetheless suspected a possible suicide attempt and followed up on her.

Of course, her window of opportunity for time travel was always open. However, it took her a long time to realize that. The choking flood of grief eventually receded. Her hope of time travel resurfaced; it was not washed away with it. The past wasn't going anywhere. Fortunately, the thought of avenging his death was out of the question as well. The monsters, her would-be prey, turned out to be students, her son's age. They had been identified, apprehended and protected by the law.

Her *desire* for revenge, nonetheless, surfaced again sometimes too. Thus, the first few weeks were unbearable to Delora as she struggled to get back to living with purpose. She continued to receive condolences and visits from well-wishing strangers who wanted to let her know they were there for her if she needed anything. But they couldn't help, not really. What she *needed* was to go back in time and save her son.

Of course she didn't respond with that. Delora couldn't make that requirement sound serious. She was not the type of ask for help in any event, and she was very much out of her comfort zone. She missed her son, her privacy and the solitude of her life on her boat. Rather than human connection, she longed for communion with the pod.

After the funeral and the buzz around town subsided, Delora decided she was able to return to her research, albeit alone now. She had made a huge step forward, but she was only human. She continued to review events, doubting and second-guessing herself. During the next six months of withdrawal from human society and an intense focus on work, time passed slowly for her. She had plenty of opportunity to reflect on time travel and her experience. It was possible that she had come close to death and when her life flashed before her eyes it *seemed* like time travel, but in fact was vivid memory recall. Rather than draw a conclusion, which she knew would be unscientific, she was ultimately comfortable with not knowing for sure what had occurred.

She had hoped her experience would have resulted in a dramatic shift in communication between her and the pod, but she was most disappointed that was not the case. Complete understanding between human and orca would be essential for another try. Otherwise Akenehi would simply either save her again or, she supposed, even let her drown. Consequences of another failed attempt might even result in being diagnosed suicidal and so on. That would not do. She was committed to keeping Alvar's memories alive and was not ready to risk her life and repeat failure in the water, no matter how interesting or exhilarating.

Akenehi and her clan had continued to show interest in her since the event, but it was not noticeably heightened. Delora began singing for her own enjoyment during her days out at sea as the sound of her improved range pleased her. The clan showed a bit more interest in her when she sang the upper range notes, but that was about it. She studied other cetaceans in the area. In addition to her usual acoustic recordings, she noted population numbers, migration and surface behaviors. There had been occasional sightings of sperm whales and she very much wanted to observe them up close, but the last few months had been pretty barren of sightings of that species.

Occasionally she was treated to interesting interactions with a few of the dolphin species. It never failed to lift her spirits when she was accompanied by bow riding dolphins. One day in particular, two dolphins amused themselves with Delora and her equipment. They were interested and playful and she noted it was a male and female pair. She knew the species was not monogamous, but observed their exuberance and affection with each other. After a while they got bored with her and swam off, surfacing together. She continued to watch them as they jumped in unison, so sleek and magnificent.

Her solitary trips to sea, which included singing, swimming and exposure to plenty of sunshine, rather than any human conversation or pharmaceutical, were bringing her out of her sadness. She had been profoundly altered by her experience and she was still missing her son so much. Her personal journal entries sounded the same.

*I had a wonderful, life changing experience, but my son is still gone. Happiness and despair. They tend to cancel each other out and overall I'm feeling rather flat. I sing and swim and that really gives me a lift. I am working on a communication breakthrough but nothing yet. And here I am, day after day.*

She wrote much on her frustration of her inability to actually communicate with her new family, the pod. She wanted not only to thank them for saving her life, but to explain all that was in her soul and be one of the clan. Delora felt connected to everything, but her thoughts were still stuck in her own head, and the more she tried to put them into words, the sillier it all sounded. She decided to write Akenehi a letter, not only about Alvar, and certainly not about time travel, but one explaining why she felt such a close connection to her. She actually gave it to her; fully cognizant it could not be read or understood. The exercise was therapeutic and for Delora alone.

She wrote:

*Dear Akenehi:*

*Whether you intended to or not, you saved me. As a result, I feel even more deeply connected to you and I love you as my own family. You, Akenehi, are a great mystery to me—beautiful, powerful, loving and intelligent. My presence in your world is my attempt to learn who you are. I respect you without knowing you, and admire your natural physical appearance, which next to mine humbles me so.*

*When I try to conceptualize you in your world, so unknown to me, much is a void. I fill that void with myself and what I have experienced with my own kind. I have carefully observed and collected data, but still know so little of who you are to each other. I hypothesize similarities and differences between our species. Who I am at this moment is the sum total of so many constantly shifting variables—genetic, educational, environmental, physical. One of my favorite sayings is "Change is the only true constant in the universe". That being said, I know as soon as I have written this down, I will have changed in some way. This helps me understand that what I want will continue to elude me. That said, I am fairly positive that today, and every day of my human life,*

*I want to be one of you, one with you.*

*I know that in the process of daily living I have already started to forget details about my own life as well as my son's, so I am in a constant state of loss. As a student of biology and organic beings I know our bodies are always fighting to live, cycling even as we sleep in energy expenditure, cellular damage, death and repair—and that ultimately our bodies will lose that battle. I hope that some part of Alvar and me will survive as I have always longed for us to be Orcas, living in your memory, having successfully shared ourselves with you. I am writing this letter to you, merely an observer, a cross-section of a human existence in perpetual change. Hopefully someday, I will not be merely an observer, but will have transformed from human to Orca, in memory or otherwise.*

*I want you to know the experiences I gained the day you saved me. For example, I feel more and more that my human body is a holding pen for a wild piece of something that is much larger. But I am interpreting those experiences from my old, learned human perspective. My body is a "me", a "self", and it feels like "one" although I learned in biology that it is actually a symbiotic colony of specialized single-celled organisms, self-organized into sophisticated systems. My thoughts flow out via human neurons, with interconnections numbering greater than stars in the galaxy. Every living body, in essence, is a universe within itself, of life and energy and thought, and it works always to survive. Our neurons are organic batteries. Once all of my batteries fail in unison there will be no more of my own unique memories. When my batteries die, my thoughts, my perception of self, and more importantly, the sweetest memories of Alvar will be lost. Now that he is gone I must live.*

*Or so I thought.*

*I gained the sense that his essence is there; it does not require my persistent human existence. The ocean, perhaps the universe also, is a library of memory, and now my human language will fall short of what I am trying to convey. So I will sing to you, and you may understand that, instead.*

*Another of my favorite sayings is: "The energy never dies". I think of Alvar. Energy cannot be created or destroyed, and it flows and moves and ex-*

*changes itself. I know I have already consumed the energy of many other creatures, requiring their deaths, and in turn my cells have died many deaths. But the energy has persisted and transferred to me and the environment. Their energy came to me, joined with me. My current body is a copy made from the instructions of the original DNA supplied at my conception, an event now long past, with those molecules long since replaced. Even after my neurons die en masse, my body's energy will dissipate and move on. That energy will continue on to the end of the universe itself, shifting places and forms. That knowledge also serves as a consolation that some essence of Alvar will always* be. *My human memories of him seem irrelevant in relation to that vast existence, but I want them to go on just the same.*

*My body is in constant repair and change, always renewing, yet I feel a continuity of self throughout my life. I wonder where this "I", or constant feeling of being "one" comes from. Is it the universe itself that looks out through my temporary eyes to view itself, and that is the spark or spirit I mistakenly think as separate?*

*In a way, the universe keeps itself company, copes with the insane eternity, by creating the illusion of death. One being is identifiable to one location and another being at its own location. But all belong to that same ocean made up internally of the same water—the fundamental essence of the universe's energy. All boundaries between locations smear upon close scrutiny, and the defining edges fade to blend seamlessly with space into an imperceptible gradation with the oneness of everything. The ocean of energy then suffers all death, loves all its children and all children come from it, trying life and enjoying its temporary successes and despairing in its temporary failures regardless of right or wrong.*

*I can only imagine how strange my ideas might be to an Orca! Or not.*

*After my experience, I have been more inclined to trust my instincts. I have been taught they are vague and lesser developed senses. The ocean is dense and contains much more physical data than the thin air I live in as a human. It seems to me that you have developed senses with an ability to read some of its contents. While that library of the ocean is open to your senses; it is a foreign planet to me. Differences in our levels of awareness are analo-*

*gous to eye development across species. Simple single cell organisms do not have eyes as mine or yours. Ours are multi-cellular and complex. Theirs are little more than photo-sensitive spots, but they can sense light and it enables a response in the behavior of the organism. Their eye spots can 'read' some of the data the light contains, but our eyes are more developed and we can detect much more detail. My instincts and perceptions of the ocean's information compared to your cognitive ability are analogous to primitive eye spots compared to our eyes. I have gained that knowledge as well.*

*You and I, Akenehi, are like a right and left arm of the same body. Like a human neuron of the universe and an Orca neuron of the universe. We, all living beings, are also perhaps the neurons of God, more than of our single universe. What we know, the universe knows. What we see, the universe sees. When one neuron goes silent another still fires as long as life goes on. One perspective is lost, but others persist. While each might feel apart and alone, the universe nevertheless always connects each into a whole, without limitation of space or time. I want you to know my perspective on this and I don't know why. But it is vital to me.*

*Thank you again for tolerating my presence in your world and for the interest you have shown me and the knowledge I have gained from you. Thank you for all you did for Alvar. He loved you. I think you know that. Thank you for saving my life. I hope you felt, as I do, that that act enhanced our bond beyond friendship to family. I hope that can be even further deepened someday.*

*Love, Delora*

The next meeting with the pod, Delora carefully rolled up the letter, singing and feeling better than she felt in months, and inserted it through a hexagon at the end of her C-cage model. She placed it into the net and extended the wand. The clan scanned the ball with the object inside of it. Delora had not expected to record what she saw as a private ritual for her own healing, but she wished she had now. The vocalizations were noticeably excited. She remembered Alvar's success and realized she had just duplicated it. She wished he could have been there.

Delora had suspected there might have been a direct connection with the

C-cage and her experience, but had not taken it back out during these months until the day she presented her letter to Akenehi. It was time to explore responses with further exposure to this particular item.

**Orca: AKENEHI**

Akenehi and the others had taken careful note of the resonance and some interesting parallels from their encounters with Alvar's molecule model. The Orca brain was able to produce and comprehend acoustic information and use it as a tool in much the same way humans used their opposable thumbs. A human manufactures a fishing line, net, and applies bait, all to catch a fish. An Orca would produce a series of sounds to locate, scan and even stun them if necessary.

An Orca was to sound, as a human was to technology.

Delora had unknowingly exposed Akenehi to the scientific method as it applies to human made objects. Akenehi was a quick study and was able to integrate newly acquired resonances with songs and ancient purposes that had been handed down to her, and lessons learned through her own long, eventful life. While Delora was studying and observing them, so Akenehi was also studying and observing her.

Akenehi was beginning to suspect that the presence of the long jaw and his echo-bursts may have contributed to the successful results of Delora's vocal mechanism. On the other fin, it was possible it was a random success, and Akenehi had no special modification capabilities whatsoever. But Delora's improvement was real and noticeable, at least to Orcas. The clan was encouraged with the vocal modification, but Akenehi was extremely impatient; because if she was not able to modify the hearing, it was basically useless.

Akenehi strongly suspected that the land squid who no longer accompanied Delora was gone forever. His disappearance coincided with Delora's illness, and they guessed correctly that he had died. All indications confirmed to Akenehi, in full possession of her own strong maternal instinct, that he was indeed the female land squid's young. The clan acted accordingly. They sang healing songs of empathy and hope usually reserved for Orca mothers who had experienced the death of a very young calf. Akenehi regretted that Delora could not understand fully and participate; it would have enlivened her greatly. They tried to visit her as often as they could when she was in their area, having called out to them, but scarcity of prey could not always afford them much time.

Akenehi felt anxious, as she did when a violent storm was approaching. She did her best to prepare the clan, especially the youngest members, but for what, she had no idea. Delora had not presented them with the object again, and frankly Akenehi didn't feel it was necessary, but it definitely corresponded with her uneasiness. She, at least, had the complex harmonics soundly mastered. She wondered if her agitation meant she was undetectably ill and would be leaving them soon. She considered letting the clan try modification on her, a simple fin modification only, which, if failed, would cause little effect on her life, but she could hear clearly they weren't quite that ready. So the clan practiced with simple fish modifications, with limited and erratic success. Yes, thought Akenehi; the long jaw knew. Nothing in the ocean was ever hidden from a long jaw. He must have done something.

They were much occupied on a daily basis with family, care and teaching of the young, hunting and sheer entertainment. The six months passed relatively uneventfully as far as experimental results were concerned. Akenehi admitted that perhaps Orca-kind did not, on their own, possess the ability to achieve the greatness the ancient songs had claimed. Luckily for her clan, Akenehi possessed a rare gift, a truth-seeking open mind.

**Sperm Whale: BROUGH**

Eventually, Brough came across a pod of less familiar Masters. None of them knew exactly where Param was at present, but they shared clicks that she was traveling with two older males making their way to colder water for an important, yet undetailed, purpose. Brough knew the general way and so oriented himself in Param's presumed direction. He sent out the occasional coda and clicks, but he had no desire to be harassed by Orcas or humans. Orcas always seemed to be listening for the distinctive sounds of long jaw young and vulnerable. He didn't consider himself vulnerable, but he wasn't going to invite any sport either. Humans were unpredictable and even more lethal when they were so inclined. He continued on his way, read the ocean current and contents, hunted squid and listened for a response to his calls.

Many months later he went to the aid of a solitary mother and young calf. As they came in range, the mother, who also happened to be a daughter of Param, broke her silence to call out to him urgently, requesting his protection. Of course he complied. He changed course immediately and swam at top speed, following her clicks. She emitted hers sporadically while her calf stayed close, keeping up. She used a strategy of efficient click spacing, so he knew they were heading for him but also provided updates to the predator-evasive course she and her calf were taking. When they came into physical presence, Brough was briefly welcomed as they exchanged introductory clicks, but then her clicks became information rich.

He received terrible images of her family pod coming under sudden human attack. A young male and one of their pregnant females had been violently killed and removed from the ocean. There was nothing any of them could have done. One male had accompanied her and the calf during deep dive to escape. The same human vessel had pursued them, so he went off to draw them away from her and the calf, leaving them alone as they stayed submerged, swimming fast, and fortunately coming within Brough's faint beacon. In her retreat, she had listened intently to clicks conveying that others were successfully eluding the hunters, and some were staying behind submerged in the general area, in the event their relatives' bodies would somehow be returned to the ocean and to them.

Brough committed the images and information from her clicks to his own memory. Brough learned the mother and calf's signature clicks and memorized those as well. He would inform Param of these events upon finding her. He accompanied them for days, taking a necessary detour back toward warmer waters. The calf was nervous and distraught. The adults comforted him and stayed within distance of easy physical touch. His mother reinforced to the calf that with Brough's help they were quite safe.

Brough occasionally scanned the ocean for a very specific item, remaining quiet for safety's sake much of the time. Eventually he found it. He stunned the large fish and ate it. The mother knew this game, all Masters did, and she had taught it to the calf. The calf recognized it instantly and cheerfully turned to echo blast the journey of the fish from Brough's mouth to stomach. The young Master had enough natural ability to image the fish clearly inside his protector. From previous experience playing this game he knew that fish had been selected because it had very recently eaten. The challenge was to determine correctly if there was a fish within that fish and so on. It encouraged very detailed scans. "Fish in a fish in a fish in a Master!" was the returning echo. Brough recalled when a brush with death taught him to fully understand the deeper meaning, the cycling of life, taught by that game. In this lesson, the young Master that day experienced the leap in comprehension that he, too, was consumable, and the cycle did not stop with him.

Eager for another game to pass the time as they traveled, Brough lead them to the ocean floor and scanned until he found a suitable subject. Bones, all belonging to a single creature, scattered about an area. The object of the game was to have the young echo scan the remains, and then locate a living specimen. Upon correct identification, he must scan it and determine it if is benign or potentially harmful. Brough suspected this would keep the young Master's thoughts occupied for some time, as he strategically selected bones of a less common species. Brough, certain there were no Orcas within a great distance, gave the signal it was safe to begin the search with "What creature?" The young calf was happily amused with this game for the next few hours.

During that time, Param's daughter shared information about her mother's interest in the extremely fine detail she imaged from varying layers of the vast ocean floor; from the soft, newer top to the older, compacted deep solids, embedded with tiny bones and solid trapped shadows of long dead creatures. The ocean water held memories and living data, and these were read by all Masters. The surface of the ocean floor was also read by all as it was virtually transparent to their natural echolocation. However, reading the increasingly subtle mysterious memories entombed deep down past the transparent floor was only an ability of the most practiced and skilled Aware Masters. Param was the oldest living of those capable.

Param's daughter last echo scanned her mother as Param left the family pod with two accompanying males with a dual purpose. The three were on a long journey to conduct detailed scans of the colder ocean floors, and also study the small, almost undetectable tardigrades they would find there. Param had recently worked out that an ocean-wide event was imminent, perhaps devastating and terrible, perhaps creative and wonderful. It might affect the entire ocean and all of its creatures.

Eventually Brough, mother and calf heard the distant calls of another larger pod. They met up, exchanged greetings and information. Mother and calf would continue on with the guaranteed protection and social interaction of that larger group. The pod desired Brough to join them, but he clicked his intent to continue on his own way. Brough, mother and calf tenderly stroked each other goodbye. The Aware Master departed, with even more urgent purpose, heading toward colder waters.

## CHAPTER FOUR

### Human: LIAM

Aside from Delora, Johnny's mother was the most traumatized over the tragedy of Alvar's death. She became obsessed with the desire to make right what could never possibly be. She felt she had done a horrible job as a mother; had failed her son, let her family fall to ruins, and now Johnny was likely going to end up in jail with this horrible memory to carry with him the rest of his life. When she phoned her brother, Liam, and told him what had happened, he also knew that he had failed his family. Before this happened, he knew his sister had family problems, but he thought she had been getting them sorted out on her own. Without being asked, he decided to return to his hometown and be a good substitute father figure to his nephews and support to his sister. When his sister told him the victim and his mother were cetacean researchers, he felt vested for that reason as well. He was a marine biologist himself and had always felt a sort of familial bond to others who shared his interest and commitment. Liam knew the mother's feelings would likely be negative toward him, and did not want to cold-call her or meet her by chance.

Almost six months to the day of her son's tragic death, Delora's doctor paid her a house call. He was still suspicious she might harm herself. She continued to be noticeably withdrawn and resisted even his skilled attempts at drawing out detailed information of her experience on the boat. She would never talk about how she found Alvar that morning, or how she had come to be cold and wet in the boat when the Coast Guard found her. Delora calmly reassured him she was fine and yet refused to go into any further detail. He was there that day with a specific purpose, however; to set up an introduction to Liam McElroy, who he had known for decades.

The doctor had met Liam when he was just a frightened boy with a broken arm. He had watched him grow into a decent adult, one with extensive experience with, and knowledge of, cetaceans. He suspected that mutual interest could help bring Delora out of her shell. Liam had specifically asked the doctor to introduce them. They both knew that Delora would resent the fact that Liam was Johnny's uncle, but the doctor felt that establishing such a dialogue would be a crucial step to her recovery.

Liam prepared for their first meeting by reading Delora's published articles, which he found insightful and pioneering. He would not have to feign admiration for her. Aside from their mutual interest in cetaceans, and her son's horrible death, Liam had found little information about her.

When Delora initially resisted meeting anyone new, for fear of enduring yet another conversation reliving her despair and hearing now-familiar condolences, the doctor informed her Liam had requested the meeting himself and that they had a mutual background in dolphin and whale studies. He also, wisely, told her he was a relative of Johnny's who had recently moved back to town, so she knew that going into the meeting. He knew Delora well enough to use the approach of doing a favor for a colleague or an admirer of her work. She could be coaxed out of herself if there was an opportunity to discuss her findings. Frankly, Delora was not yet willing to consider forgiveness, and it would be uncomfortable if this man were to request it, but she felt it would be baseless to extend blame to anyone other than the three young men directly involved. She decided she would be introduced without pre-determined hostility and was ready to counter any unwelcomed requests.

It seems the doctor had written the perfect prescription after all. When Delora laid eyes on Liam McElroy she felt her breath catch just a bit, her lips part and her pupils involuntarily dilate as she took him in. He seemed so very familiar, in a warm and comfortable way. When the doctor talked about him, somehow she'd expected a twenty-something clean-shaven youth. He was actually around her age and disarmingly casual, very familiar and unpretentious in clothing and demeanor. He was not supermodel gorgeous. No, rather, he had a physical *presence* that caught her completely off guard and set her senses on alert. It seemed he was radiating energy and a *rhythm* that was in tune with Delora's. And this energetic presence immediately intrigued her. She also deeply felt that "click" of mutual interest she had only felt once before—one that is rarely a figment of one's imagination or wishful thinking.

"Very pleased to finally meet you. I've read your papers and greatly admire your work," Liam blurted out as he shook her hand gently. Rather than letting go immediately, he placed his other hand comfortably on top. "I am so sorry about your son. So very sorry".

He was so natural and sincere; she liked and trusted him already. And he looked so damned familiar. She tried to place him. Then she remembered.

Two days before this meeting she'd caught a glimpse of him walking across a street downtown. He had crossed just in front of her as she was stopped at a stoplight. He had a *rhythmic* spring to his step and movement that felt somehow contagious to her, like she would want to dance if she were to physically touch him. She couldn't help but smile as she watched him move. A quick series of honks from the driver behind her snapped her out of it. The light had changed and she was still watching him, lost in her reverie. At the noise, Liam turned around. They caught sight of each other as she slowly pulled forward. Many women might have been embarrassed, but not Delora. She was glad he had seen her. As she slowly pulled away, she looked back in her rearview mirror. He was still watching after her, smiling.

She'd felt alive, more like her old self, all day.

Now, Liam was sitting with the doctor and they were all having a very friendly, comfortable conversation. Delora had risen to fetch them all something to drink and he looked around, noticing a picture on the side table and wondering if it would be a good idea to inquire if it was a picture of her and her son. Then his breathing halted and his mouth dropped open as he examined the image. He knew that face. He knew both of those faces.

"Is this you?" he called out to her in the kitchen as he scrutinized Delora's photo and the youthful features looking back at him. He recalled a younger "Lori". She was older now, a little bit heavier, her hairstyle was different but she was still healthy, with a familiar glow despite her aura of mourning. He was more altered than she by far. He had facial hair now, and some gray peppering his dark hair, and he too had weathered and filled out as age does to a body. "It is you! My God! Lori…oh no, no…"

The woman preparing tea in the kitchen was the same lover and soul mate he had met during his youth as he demonstrated for cetacean rights and traveled overseas years ago. He also realized the small boy's face in the photo could have been his own at that age. He was going to ask where the boy was now, then he recalled in horror that he already knew that answer.

From the kitchen Delora heard Liam exclaim with emotion and heard him use the name "Lori". Only close friends from her youth and her family called her that. It was then that she recalled another face. A much younger face. And when she entered the living room and looked again at Liam, that beautiful young man looked back at her as though he'd just fallen off a cliff into ice cold water.

The doctor took this cue and left, but Liam remained with Lori.

They spent the rest of the evening catching up. Delora had some explaining to do, but Liam took full responsibility for being untraceable. Anonymity and quick movement from place to place were his strategies for success during protests that included very bold and sometimes illegal activity, as Delora knew. They spoke formally at first, comparing dates of major life events and places they had traveled to, work they had done, but then it became familiar and easily intimate as the conversation turned to Alvar.

Liam was absolutely amazed as the hours passed, at how Delora was happy and animated and full of love when she spoke of her son, explaining details of photos of their life together, artwork he had done, science projects, awards he had won and the like. He knew she was in deep mourning for him, and he finally decided he would ask, as the evening was drawing to a close, how she could put on a happy face when such a terrible loss had occurred. She answered without missing a beat, with a glow radiating from her face.

"Alvar gave me so much joy when he was alive, made me so very happy,

I carry that with me always. I may not tolerate people much, but here, where Alvar and I were a family, and out on the sea that he loved as much as I did, I'm at peace." Then she hesitated a moment, looked down at her hands as she lightly massaged her left palm, remembered the creases of Alvar's tiny palm when he was an infant. "This may sound crazy to you, but I know I will see him again, be with him again. I just *know* it."

Liam had come that evening to meet Delora to express his sympathy with her grief but left with more than enough of his own.

After that meeting, and over the next few months, Delora came to know Liam as a trustworthily confidant and capable, intelligent researcher. He was also devoted to his sister and Johnny, and felt profound remorse that he'd never had a relationship with Alvar. Despite Delora's struggle with his relationship with Johnny, there was no other possible outcome than to accept the biological father of her son as her companion in grief. She looked forward to the time they spent together and they became friends. It became harder and harder to leave his presence once she was in it.

* * * * *

One early evening Liam came over to her house unannounced, and sat her down with unconcealed agitation to tell her some news. He was considering moving.

Delora sat frozen and stunned. "You're leaving town?"

"Well." He furrowed his brow and stammered a little as he continued, "My, uh, sister, you know, is doing much better, much, *much* better these days. She is genuinely happier, anyone can plainly see. Johnny is out of detention and I feel that I need to get out of her house and…"

Delora felt suddenly desperate and fought a huge lump in her throat and cut him off mid-sentence. "I have a hard time verbalizing my deepest feelings, as you know…but with the empty house now and all…" She looked down at her thumbnail and picked at it with distracted determination.

Liam accepted the interruption, sat quietly for several long moments, watching for clues to her true feelings and waiting for her to continue.

Delora knew she had to find her courage, risk flat out rejection and the end of this precious relationship and just tell him how she felt. “Look, Liam, you’re my best friend. And more than that, so much more. I’ve developed feelings for you.” She looked into his eyes. Maybe that was too much too soon. She looked down again, leaned toward him, but didn’t look up at him. She gripped her seat cushion hard with both hands. *Steady, Delora, you’re making him nervous and making a fool of yourself!* She inhaled, then spoke as plainly as she could, “What I’m trying to say…is…I know you’re a grown-up and need your own place away from your sister’s, to get back to your life. I guess I thought this might happen, but please…don’t…leave.”

Liam watched all of her movements and expressions with affection. She was beginning to fight back tears and he was afraid he would soon do the same in empathy if he didn’t speak up. He smiled at her unconsciously, then caught himself. She had initiated a more serious conversation and he was annoyed at himself for grinning at her, but he just couldn’t help it. He tried to remember the scenario he had envisioned, but it was obviously not going to play out as rehearsed. He didn’t want to rush her into a commitment either, but they both knew they’d had a relationship of sorts for most of their lives.

“Listen, Lori…”

At that, Delora looked up at him, positively mortified. “I’m sorry. I shouldn’t have that. If you need to go…”

Liam couldn’t help but chuckle at this and shook his head side to side. “No, no, not all. I love it that you just say what you mean. I’ve wanted to say something since the moment I knew I’d found you again. You are the love of my life; you always have been and are even more so now. I want us to share our lives, right now, for as long as possible.”

Delora released her chokehold on the cushion, lightly shaking off the muscle tension in her hands and looked straight into his eyes, released the breath she had been holding and broke out into her hugest smile. “Oh, thank God. I thought I was losing you! You can move in now, Liam. Right now. I mean it. Stay the night.” Delora drew back just a bit and looked confused, because first, she actually said that out loud, second, she actually meant it and third, Liam was chuckling,

He gestured toward the front door "Well... I brought a few things over, they're in the car, hope you don't mind."

The *tempo* was fast but it was in perfect time.

They sat in silence for a moment, just smiling at each other. Grief and recovery had demanded a respectful distance until now. Making perfect music required being on beat. Their hearts were pounding with it and it felt wonderful.

A few minutes later, the oven timer sounded, breaking the tempo of their first dance since they were overseas. They felt twenty years old again.

"Dinner! There's a bottle of Riesling in the fridge."

Liam released his partners hand gently and noticed his face was starting to ache from smiling so big. He went into the kitchen and opened the fridge. "Good choice. Half empty...but a good choice. Where's yours?"

"I have another in the pantry...here." She pushed past two reds to the white. "I like it room temp anyway." Delora hadn't felt so happy at home since Alvar was alive. She grabbed two oven mitts out of a drawer.

During dinner she watched with humor and deepening affection as he wolfed down her cooking with genuine surprise and frequent comments over the fact that he actually liked it and could physically chew and swallow it. As the evening progressed, Delora felt occasional waves of terror as she realized she was putting her future happiness in his hands, and that was a crushing burden to impose on anyone. It might drive him away if she didn't get it under control. But she had to fully own that she had been nearly dead inside since she lost Alvar, and with Liam she felt satisfied with her human life and love again.

Liam was not sorry he had fallen in love with Delora all over again. Not only did she manage to make the best casserole he had ever tasted, but it was the most interesting evening of conversation he had ever participated in. Delora shared personal moving anecdotes about Alvar's birth and precious babyhood she had never told anyone else. She shared the most details to date on her experience the day she found Alvar dead, and how she had been spiritually transformed by her deepened bond with Akenehi and her pod, and even her newly improved singing voice.

She sang for him for the first time. As she serenaded him, he felt the hair on his arms and back of his neck involuntarily stand on end. Tears came to his eyes. She was a true talent. She admitted there was no before recording to compare it with, as she never sang prior to the change, because she simply had no desire, no ability. But she told him there was great improvement.

Liam, a musician himself, was intrigued. He shared his love of the cello for the first time with her and promised to serenade her in return very soon. Liam was a history buff, knew facts, statistics and wars in the way some obsessed over in sports. That was one thing they did not share. Delora had absolutely no desire to relive the horrors of war. She was the type to turn off a war program, turn away from violent images of political conflict, and avoid the first half of the news, as it contained politics and violence. They both longed to witness the admittedly impossible during their own lifetimes—the absolute eradication of all such violence and wasted human spirit.

The official first evening in their shared home, full of sweet Riesling, small affectionate kisses, slow dancing, music, desires and ideas on improving humanity, interest in cetaceans, and especially remembering their son, reinforced a comfort between them that Liam absolutely knew would only be found with her.

**Sperm Whale: BROUGH**

Brough came within reading distance of powerful clicks from Param and her companions as they deep scanned the ocean floor. He did not need to call out to them to announce his approach, they knew. His proximity was already obvious in their practiced echoes. Although it was day at the surface, at that depth it was almost completely dark, and they relied totally on sound. Adhering to protocol, they exchanged individual and pod identification clicks as they came within physical presence. Param timed her greeting so the signals did not interfere with her own returning echoes of the ocean floor. She continued to deep scan the floor as they greeted each other. This was not rudeness, nor was it showing off her singular ability. It was efficient and informative as they all benefited from the returning data as well.

During the initial greeting, he noted all three stomachs were full of squid. They noted his was as well. Prey thrived here in relative abundance and was it not for the cold; they would have wanted to remain. He was grateful he had so many successful hunts along the way. His energy was excellent and he was able to happily tolerate the thin layer of chill the icy water offered. All were physically comfortable, content.

He was sorry their lighthearted exchange would soon be consumed by the disquieting scenes he had come so far to share. They had already sensed his tension and were waiting for what was coming. Wasting no time after polite introduction, Brough, in a quick series of clicks, efficiently detailed the stories of attack and death on Param's family. Characteristic of aged Aware Masters, she experienced her profound grief with peace and acceptance. She was very grateful for the protection he provided her daughter and offered him acceptance in their small pod.

Brough accepted graciously, but continued hastily with other urgent details he had swum for months and expended so much energy to share. As it turned out, his information was indeed appreciated; it contributed a critical piece to a puzzle Param had been working on for almost a full decade. The four Aware exchanged clicks about Brough's memorized interaction between Human and Orca, the presence of the sacred bit, and the much larger scale object which mirrored the shape of the microscopic one. They thoroughly clicked Param's conclusions based on the fossil records she had been examining and the ocean temperatures and decreases in number of almost all its creatures they had noted. Relevant memories of generations of Masters long dead, whose fine records of certain events were passed down, were carefully reviewed and discussed. It was detailed eons ago, but certain Masters had recorded a relationship between Orca and sacred bits. An unspecified result had been highly in favor of Orcas and disastrous for Masters.

In less than a day, these four Aware Masters had reviewed masses of shared memory and relevant physical data in their surroundings; knowledge and meaning elusive to all except those possessing the finest Aware skills. Thanks to information Brough had provided, large voids of uncertainty were now filled with actual occurrences and heretofore nonsensical data was at least partially comprehended. The puzzle was nearing a solution; as in the game the scattered bones were now identified, and the creature was not conclusively benign. Param and her two companions determined Brough should begin his return journey immediately and they would return to warmer waters themselves soon. Until they found each other again, he must seek further detailed scans of these events, if indeed they were to be repeated, and collect and processes as much data as possible.

Reluctantly, Brough also shared his read that the whole interaction between human, Orca and sacred bit, surprising as it had been, contained novel echo variations and fascinating fluid movements that seared an exceedingly pleasant memory within him. None of the other three Aware could offer explanation or comfort. Param reminded them, however, that they all knew that danger and death maintained a positive attraction as well as a fearsome repulsion. She reminded him of the profound respect they held for the intelligence of the giant squid; their mesmerizing physiological detail; their graceful fluid swirls of complex turbulence from their movements that were so pleasing to scan and recall—yet they must be killed and consumed or Masters themselves could not be. She announced after consideration there could be another possibility, and it fit elegantly as part of the solution to her puzzle.

As Brough started his long journey back to warmth and destiny, he recalled "fish in a fish in a fish in a Master". He did not comprehend until his meeting with Param, and reading her data from the deep floor, that all Masters could be collectively consumed, ended for all time. All Masters in an Orca. All Masters in a human. No, it must not be.

<u>CHAPTER FIVE</u>

**Human: DELORA and LIAM**

Delora had been transformed by her experience of Alvar's death, and with the Orcas that fateful day, and she worked it all into her career. She confided many more research details, interpretations and hypotheses to Liam and to her journal and to no one else. Working again with an equally committed and experienced partner offered the promise of spectacular publishable results. Liam reminded her it was poor science to "want" an outcome, and she knew that. His objectivity made him even more appreciated out in the field.

Liam, deeply in love with her, wanted to make sure she was safe and to keep her professionally on track. He intended to protect her as much as he could if she engaged in dangerous risks out in the field, and to objectively counter any experience she might misinterpret. He knew she was subject to wishful thinking. Liam had to admit he secretly shared her wish for time travel, as he was working through his own feelings of mourning for a son he did not know he had. When Delora talked about going back to save Alvar (she would not have been comfortable with that confession to anyone other than Liam) he felt she was definitely being wishful, but he hoped she might be right. Heck, he had sure seen enough time travel movies to know it was a desired, if not possible, idea. More than anything, he was intrigued by her spiritual experience with the Orcas, and felt that was reasonably attainable. And if there was any chance she could succeed in reproducing that, he wanted to be the test subject.

The months that followed were the best of his human life. Delora and Liam moved out of the house Alvar had died in, and into a cozy, rustic, two bedroom cabin by the water. It had a screened-in front porch that spanned the width of the cabin, a tiny four season sunroom off the back facing mature trees with just enough room for a couple of comfortable reading chairs and a lamp (this was Delora's favorite part of the place, and it sold her on the property), and its own private dock. This feature sold Liam on the place, as Delora's boat would conveniently transport them out to sea, where they would both now carry out trials for their research. They were wonderful times for Delora too, but they were not the best. Those belonged to Alvar.

Delora decorated every room, except one, with some kind of cetacean theme. Liam had WWII-themed art, a helmet and other knick-knacks, but Delora banished those to the garage. War was not her. Cetaceans definitely were. They were Liam too. The kitchen lent itself easily to Orca. Black appliances, white cabinets, black and white Orca prints and kitchen towels, and even Orca salt and pepper shakers. The living area was general cetacean. The bookshelf filled with the topic. Blue paint on the walls, dolphin and whale art and knickknacks crowded any available wall or shelf space. Friends who knew she collected had helped enhance the variety over the years, not only in type of cetacean, but in type of collectable. Delora had dolphin and whale themed pillows, throw blankets, coffee mugs, even lamps along with the centerpiece of the room—a glass coffee table supported by a dolphin sculpture underneath.

The one room in the house not decorated this way was the second bedroom. Delora called it Alvar's room, and Liam agreed it should be so. It was the official guest room but it contained Alvar's favorite science books, pictures of him on the wall, and some of his clothes in the closet Delora couldn't bear to part with as well as his molecule model. There were a few random nights when she couldn't sleep, and Delora would leave Liam asleep in bed and go into Alvar's room. It wasn't the same bed he died on, but she would lay on it and look at the spherical carbon-60 molecule model she placed on the bedside table, in much the same position as it was when she had found him that morning. She did not feel she was punishing or tormenting herself in these actions, although she would sometimes cry. On the contrary, she felt he was closer to her at these moments, and she would stare at the model and find it soothing, not disturbing, until she fell asleep.

On one such night she started to doze off and there was Alvar. He was writing on the kitchen table with a paintbrush. He read back what he was writing.

*"A quantum event, as you know, Mom, is mysterious and exciting. Resonating strings, quantum level reality. I'm there. We live there together. Continue your discovery. It's okay, everything is going to be fine. Don't worry about me, Mom. Quantum...pop into and out of existence...reality...sequence has no meaning...the process and story of the creation of the universe itself is there."*

She fell into a deep sleep. Alvar was singing a lecture he had just written to her. Music played. Orca whistle became strings. Whale echolocation bursts became percussion; all accompanied him. She sang his lyrics, repeating them like a refrain.

*"A molecule, in nature found; Common in space, vacuum, no sound*
*Exhibiting wave and very safe; common in dirt, your garden now*
*Powerful, changing your body; with sound*
*Alter your voice, you take its place; with sound*
*Common in space, vacuum, no sound; with wave with sound, you take its place"*

When she woke up, she remembered the song vividly. She tried humming it to herself, then singing, but found the range went way beyond what she could produce, even with her improved voice. She understood it completely while she was sleeping, but now that she was awake, not so much. It was a catchy, soothing tune, though, and its words haunted her like something Alvar might actually have written. She lay in bed and practiced until she had it committed to memory. It was the best ever being with Alvar again, even if it was a dream and she hoped she could force herself to have it again. It had been pure joy.

Delora told Liam about the dream duet. They worked out a version of the tune, an octave lower than she recalled in sleep, but pretty nonetheless. It was the first time they actually composed a piece of music together and it was great fun. They played off of each other's gifts harmoniously. Liam played his cello, Delora sang and thoughts of Alvar were music in their hearts.

* * * * *

"Got it." Liam nodded and they walked to the boat in silence, visualizing the day's events as they imagined they might occur. As they were boarding Liam said, "Alvar was a brilliant kid. The books and articles he read are fascinating, especially the theoretical physics and quantum biology stuff. I feel I've gotten to know him by reading them too. I get the science."

Delora stopped, turned and squinted at him with a quizzical, skeptical expression. "Liam, my beloved, I don't think anyone fully understands what is happening at the quantum level. Nor will anyone ever. It's the uncertainty and unknown that I personally find the most exciting and promising. And the fact that it's nature, it's in us, all around us, *that's* just...perfect! No one owns it, can ever own it, any more than they can own "breathing" or "procreating". Perhaps all energy vibrates on a scale that interfaces on a quantum level and as Orcas are so skilled at acoustics...who knows, maybe they naturally perceive and control vibration nuances we aren't' even aware of? We'll identify something of the Orca behaviors that contributed to my experience, at the very least. Hell, I'll be happy if I recognize any of the harmonics from that day. I don't think the "how" or "why" will be available to us. So don't worry about getting it. Besides, a nice thing about being your own boss is that you don't have to explain yourself! Let's have a little fun!" She continued prepping the boat for launch.

Liam helped her with a heavily packed cooler. "I'll overlook that unscientific opinion as fair enough, but! I read the books, watched some You Tube videos scientists and universities are putting out about the possibility of time travel and multiple universes, and I will not dismiss your experience. And remember what the doctor said about endorphins when you mentioned how you felt afterward. That being said, you know I trust you. We're following your gut. I trust you so much I even tried your tuna casserole and it convinced *me* you can do miracles. And to this day, we have it once a week! However, jumping into the open sea amid a pod of possibly hungry Orcas with a carbon soccer ball molecule as my only peace offering? Now that I'm faced with it, sounds a bit foolhardy." Delora kept working and didn't look up at him or answer. So he continued. "Well then, if we fail but survive, at least we'll have a great experience to tell our grandchildren.'

At this Delora paused and stared deeply at him. "And if I we don't live?" When he didn't answer right away she cocked her head and squinted her eyes a bit. "Grandchildren?" She smiled at him, imagining him aged, weathered and still at her side many years from that day.

"Well, if I get eaten alive", Liam continued matter-of-factly, "then I'll stop trusting you forever. Agreed?"

Delora stared at him with a worried look on her face. "You're having doubts. You don't have to get in the water with them. If you want to experience what I did, I think it will be necessary, but that's purely a guess on my part. Getting comfortable with them in the water is what I've done, but comfort or prior experience may not be a factor at all. Who knows if what happened to me can even be replicated. You can just watch me today if that makes you more comfortable."

Liam merely shrugged. "No, I'm still good. I'm ready. You know there's no place I would rather be right now than with you, right here on this boat." He spread his arms out and pivoted his body around with a sweeping gesture. "Our own private universe!"

"Good!" Delora exclaimed. "Everything is going to be fine and I'll always have your trust!" She nodded toward the open sea. "Engage!"

Liam winked at his captain and carefully maneuvered out of the dock. Within about five minutes Liam asked Delora to take over the controls and disappeared into the tiny loo on the boat. He vomited. It was not seasickness; it was fear, plain and simple. He got it under control.

An ambitious idea had taken hold of Delora as the Coast Guard boat came toward her the day she lost her beloved son. Admittedly, she wavered, but in the end she believed she could time travel. Not just forward at a rate of one second per second as every human being did. She believed she could go backward. Back to the day Alvar died. Perhaps back further. During her experience in the water, it seemed she actually had. That had to be explored. She was a scientist but a subjective experience was not necessarily wrong. Other than Liam, she didn't want anyone joining her in her past, so subjective was just fine. If it worked, and she believed with all her soul it would, she would see Alvar again and all would be repaired. At worst, she had a great experience swimming with wild Orcas, whom she now felt closer to than her own parents.

Some physical evidence encouraged her, such as her changed voice, but that could have been a side effect of damage from the cold. She was sure her blood pressure was lower on average than it had been, and her endorphins were likely elevated. It was pleasant to simply be alive. She felt generally happy despite the horrible events of the last year, but she had to give Liam some credit for that. She was experiencing some heightened awareness and felt she understood other living beings and her surrounding physical environment more than ever.

She was a scientist, so she forced herself to come up with alternative hypotheses to explain the changes, assuming she wasn't delusional. Perhaps she had stumbled across the creation of a personal permanent bridge to another dimension or level of consciousness. Circling back to time travel, maybe the bridge could connect her to the past. Great ideas refuse to stay submerged forever.

In any event, she had hoped Liam might be able to experience the same, and it would validate her. Her hope was closer to becoming reality as he had recently consented to the experiment. But now her witness-to-be wasn't just a research partner, he was her "partner" partner and her mate. She loved him. Realizing that among other things, all of this would have to occur after overlooking the obvious human instinctive fear of swimming in a pod of giant toothed dolphins, and getting the cetaceans to understand and cooperate voluntarily, Delora accepted that more than likely her transforming spiritual experience would be limited to herself.

Months of apparatus design and testing and re-design and re-testing with long trips out to sea took its toll. She asked herself again, why was she doing this? Pursuing time travel, of all things, and putting her and Liam at risk of the elements and natural predators. The shock and anger of Alvar's passing was lessening. She was starting to heal a bit. Home with Liam was starting to feel "good enough". With it, she seemed to be losing her risk-taking resolve and questioning herself over everything Alvar used to talk about. She hated that. It seemed with the healing of her son's death her motivation to continue her research was decreasing.

Alvar would not have wanted that. Alvar was in her future if she had the intelligence and courage to go out and get him. "I wasn't wrong about the C-cage," Delora admonished herself, "or time travel to the past either. It will happen. I don't have to rush, but I can't give up either. The past is waiting and it's not going anywhere. I promise you, Alvar, I'll save you." Then she thought of Akenehi. "And I'll bring her son back too". Yes, that was her solid objective—through time travel she would change past events and thereby resurrect the dead.

So this was the day; Liam's first close encounter and hopefully, his joining. And it was a perfect one. The water was not overly choppy. The sky was clear, except for one high, smeared contrail. It was chilly but not freezing, so the boat ride would be comfortable enough. She hoped after today she would no longer be the only human soul who, as far as she knew, had experienced this phenomenon. This time, Delora kept the C-cage around her neck on a rope. If it went anywhere, she was going with it until it was time.

* * * * *

They cut the boat's engine at various places and Delora ran the recording of the greeting/call to the Orcas and waited a reasonable amount of time before moving on. No luck. At the fourth location the engine was cut off and she braced for a day of disappointment. It was as if they had gotten all dressed up but missed the wedding. Not a fin in site. Before she had a chance to play the Orca summons call, a huge lift from under the boat sent her stumbling toward the water and grabbing for purchase as she regained her balance.

Delora turned and exclaimed to a startled and crouching Liam, "What the hell was *that*? I didn't see any fins, did you?" They both searched the water surface. They stayed low, holding on, waiting for a second bump, which didn't come.

"I think we're okay, really. We're cool." Liam hoped out loud while he moved cautiously to the center of the boat, scrutinizing the water for any evidence of an object large enough to cause the jolt. He began to look around the boat and nervously fidget with random gear.

"Well." Delora tried to soothe herself with a deep exhale. "Let's turn on the camera and see if we can see anything swimming around under us." She was trying to get back on track, determined to turn this away from a fearful situation to one of joy and hope. Whatever had bumped them, it had not helped one bit. Liam looked about ready to pass out. They peered at the camera images and saw nothing, no reef, no debris, no Orcas, and thankfully, no sharks. She looked over at Liam with concern. "What's your read here, Liam?" He looked around with a worried brow and didn't offer a quick answer. "Do want to even try today now that you're totally freaked—"

Suddenly, Delora stopped mid-sentence. "There!" Several fins were approaching fast. Not steady like a shark, but surfacing and then submerging again. From the size of them they were definitely Orca. They were swimming as though in hot pursuit of something, covering a lot of water between each surfacing breath. Delora estimated they were doing about twenty-two knots, almost as fast as she'd ever witnessed.

As they approached in a matter of moments, she saw the familiar markings of Akenehi and her family. Delora was almost sure they would swim right by her, in wolf-pack determination, eager to obtain their meal. Just as they approached however, they broke formation and circled the boat, maintaining a distance of about 15 meters all around. At that moment, right beside them, Akenehi, with her massive, sleek black and white head glimmering like glass sparkling in the sun, brought her full head straight up with her eyes above water, spyhopping, deliberately and quickly surveying the interior of the boat. She dove. Then she jumped, whole body visible, out of the water, and dove back head first, slapping the water mightily with her tail. A huge banging sound resulted and the boat rocked in response. They both ducked down, avoiding as much of the monstrous splash as possible, grabbed on to each other's arms and looked wildly to where the Orca had breached.

This impressive display took both Delora's and Liam's breath away. Delora whispered to Liam, "Maybe she's pissed? Or just saying hi? I don't know! Or maybe they're hunting whatever bumped us, huh?" She decided it was better to force a smile and feign levity. "She's never done that to me before. Want me to ask her what gives?"

Liam was incredulous. "You think she's pissed and you want to hang around and find out for sure? It looked like hunting behavior to me at first." At that he began to stand, shook off as much water as possible and attempted to start the boat to get out of there.

Delora protested. "Please! Just stop. Wait."

She reached for Liam's arm and pulled him back down to her. "Breath, Liam. Squeeze my hands," she instructed. It was a stress reducing behavior she had learned. After a few quiet moments passed, they slowly stood up to survey the scene, still holding and squeezing each other's' hands. Delora assessed the scene and noted Liam no longer looked frightened. Akenehi again spyhopped close to the boat, observing them with one eye. Delora noted some other Orcas were surfacing in a slow circle, maintaining a consistent distance. It was then Delora heard Akenehi give her the learned greeting call. Delora was calm and unafraid; ready for the next step. She released his arm and said evenly, "Your turn."

Liam was stunned at this command. "Turn for *what,* exactly?"

Delora let go of him, steadied herself against the gentle waves and pronounced calmly, "You said you were ready for the experience, well, that whistle you just heard was her saying hi. So stand up and say hi… Unless, of course, you don't trust her, or you've changed your mind."

Liam nervously adjusted his scuba gear. He turned toward the Orca looking at him with one eye. He whistled a fairly impressive imitation of

Akenehi's greeting.

"Very good!" Delora was pleasantly surprised. She might have thought it was Akenehi herself.

Liam turned to Delora. "*You,* I trust. Them," he jabbed the air toward where Akenehi had breached, "I thought I trusted, but now that I'm here, after that approach and tail slap…well. No freaking way. Sorry, Lori."

Delora remained calm and didn't want to force him. Still, she urged, "Look at my face. Do I seem scared to you?"

Liam noticed Akenehi was no longer spyhopping and saw a few other fins around, but they were all calmly swimming. "No, no, you don't seem scared. But I'm the one on his way into the water."

Delora offered evenly, "I'll go in with you, then, but it won't be necessary." He still hesitated. It was time to give him a shove and snap him out of it. "Unless you've changed your mind, no more words, just go now, before they get bored with us and leave."

Liam prepared himself. "I must be insane." and, having already properly geared up, he looked at the spherical model around Delora's neck and remembered they'd agreed he should have it with him. "Here, give me that damn thing." Delora transferred the rope from her neck to his and adjusted it so it hung in front of him. Satisfied he had something that offered protection he plopped clumsily over the side of the boat.

He was an expert swimmer and recovered easily from the initial shock of cold, then pushed out a few small strokes. He looked back at Delora, who was now watching him in earnest. She whispered out over the water, which he heard with clarity, "It's okay, it's okay. You'll be okay". He noticed she had the life preserver on a rope in her hands, at the ready. He submerged and swam away from the boat a bit further. He looked around and realized he was surrounded by Orcas who had moved in much closer to him. Each Orca was about the size of a bus, and he mused he would fit easily head first and whole into any of their mouths. They vocalized in high pitch squeaky tones that faded over his hearing range and back in again, interspersed with several quick successive echolocation bursts as they examined him.

They were terrifyingly massive, but behaved gently as they swam in even closer to him. Akenehi came in so close he could have reached out to touch her. She focused her scan and vocalizations on him and he could feel the vibrations of strong echo pulses. Although he was very curious to touch her alien skin, he decided it was best to respect her personal space, to lead by example and refrain from physical contact. He also felt it was better to start moving around lest they take him for a stupid carp and move on to more interesting interactions. Delora had coached him in advance about their individual personality traits and her prior successes in engaging their natural curiosity and told him many stories of Alvar's ability to hold their attention. Now that he was there, he felt like a deer in headlights. When Liam swam toward each of them with a swim stroke he noticed they always kept one eye on him and pulled back before he got within a few meters. He respected that and stopped reaching out.

He was astonished at the Orcas' huge teeth. Liam's stomach lurched, but he tried not to panic. He thought of himself as a cetacean expert and knew enough about Orcas and their ability to use echolocation to realize now that they could see right into his body and determine his stomach contents, his emotional state, and even perhaps see beyond the bottom of the boat to whatever Delora was doing at this moment. He waved his hands in front him, thinking absurdly that it would be recognized as some universal signal that he was cool just watching and hoped maybe he was understood. They made a circle, tooth-end toward the center where Liam now hung suspended and rather paralyzed with anticipation.

At the surface, Delora was recording vocalizations and listening in with headphones. She heard a very loud series of clicks and mistook it as unusually heavy Orca echolocation. She also recorded the first visual images with her portable underwater acoustic camera. She was thrilled with what she saw and knew she was witnessing never-before-recorded Orca behavior. The relatively calm sea and sunny skies gave her a feeling that the whole universe was helping her along. She had to make a quick decision whether to continue using the camera, as it was emitting very high frequencies that she knew would interfere with the Orca vocalizations. So she ultimately decided to cut it off and rely on her acoustic recordings and visual observations.

Delora had observed Akenehi and the occasional other come up for air, but was unable to distinguish any out-of-the-ordinary surface behavior. She did record a sudden increase in vocalizations shortly after she surfaced, and she glanced down at her recorder to make sure it was on. She was euphoric as she realized she was indeed getting this. Everything was in good working order.

The Orcas tightened their position around Liam and vocalized with practiced harmony in his direction. He thought for a fleeting moment he was about to be mistaken for a seal or some other Orca lunch item.

A persistent shock of painless hot and cold seized him. He could have boiled into vapor and frozen into a brick at the same moment and would not have minded. He would later explain this to Delora as though all of his body's heat and cold receptors were all firing and leaving absolutely no signal silent, except for pain. He perceived he was no longer confined to his body as his senses were heightened and seemed to extend out into infinity. He was surrounded by blinding light and a black creamy void as he experienced the full spectrum of all wavelengths. His brain was hyper-stimulated. No filter was in effect; all neurons were excited with signals. Liam was fully aware of all, and, like Delora, could discuss this later in detail.

He was not frightened in the least. He would have been content to stay there, just as he was, suspended in the water. It felt so familiar; like a long lost home he had forgotten and could only remember now that he was there again. No need to even breathe here.

And then the euphoria hit him. This concerned him. Was he being eaten alive and endorphins were kicking in as he died? No, he decided, not at all. He was vast and timeless and without pain and boundaries and it felt really, really fabulous. *Forget breathing, I don't need it. I can never return, I cannot go back to "Liam McElroy", it will not be possible.* Peace. Love. Joy. It was all true. But no time travel that he could determine.

It had happened. Yes. Delora was right and he understood now why she had likened the sensation to being in a blinding hurricane. Liam felt as if he had survived being atomized and was remaining in that state, dispersed by the force, surrounded by orchestrated and meaningful noise and omnipotent presences. He had joined. He lost consciousness.

Akenehi appeared at the surface, pushing Liam, and lifted him up to Delora.

At first when Delora saw Liam she believed he was dead. She was in disbelief as she scrambled to retrieve him. Surprised by Akenehi's cooperation, she had little to do as Liam was virtually floated to her. Delora felt only regret and stupidity at her urging him to go through with whatever had just happened down there. *Well, Delora*, she fumed at herself, *I hope you got the recordings that will make you famous and fund your research for a few more years.* She vowed this was the end of this line of experimentation. At that moment she believed it a total failure. Then she heard him mutter something.

* * * * *

"Hologram," Liam said as he came to. He could remember that moment before he found himself in the boat, looking up into Delora's eyes full of desperate concern, thinking the Orcas were deciding he was too stupid to play with so they were going to eat him. Then, coming fully awake, he remembered it all. The universe was the top level being. He had just transcended his human level and joined with it and at that universal level he perceived with perfect clarity. It was like a hologram.

During his studies he learned the brain was like a three dimensional hologram. When the brain is healthy and whole it contains the unique personality of an individual. There is identity and clarity. In certain cases of severe brain damage where large parts of the brain are removed or die, the personality persists, still recognizable, but is faded to varying degrees depending on the amount of damage.

He thought of a snapshot his father had taken of Liam practicing cello beside a grand piano. On top of the piano was a bust of Beethoven. If one were to tear that photo in two there would result a right half which would contain Liam and his cello and a left half that would contain the piano and the bust of Beethoven. If that image had been captured as a hologram rather than a photograph, and then torn in half, the resulting contents of each half would contain Liam, his cello, the piano and the bust—each half a full representation of the untorn whole. If each of those is further torn into smaller pieces, each would still contain all of the elements of the untorn original image, but fuzzier, and less distinct with features faded. If it were broken to smaller pieces still, the image would continue to fade until it was unrecognizable as belonging to the top level image.

As a whole, the universe was a being in and of itself. At that top level there was clarity and purpose and even identity: One. Everything in the universe was a piece while still being part of the whole, and each piece had the faded image of the whole, albeit so small a piece that only a suggestion of the oneness remained at every level. Every galaxy, every solar system, every planet, every organism, every molecule, every atom, every subatomic particle is in it, belongs to it and has the oneness permeated through it.

Liam's concept of all space and time and his place in it, his life, was never the same from that moment forward. He, like Delora, now knew beyond all doubt, that he, like everything else, was literally and deeply one with the universe. Liam no longer feared being dead, knew that energy lived all lives and died all deaths and there would be no end to the cycling, the oneness, even if there was no lingering memory of any of it. He loved and felt connected to Delora like he never dreamed possible. He knew and continued to feel Alvar's presence after that experience, and he loved him every bit as much as he did Delora. She was his soul mate, like everything was also of his soul, and from that moment forward they were bound by the universe itself.

Was it that simple? *Could this be the next step in human evolution?* he asked himself as he looked up at her and saw her face framed by blue sky and light. *Can peace and happiness and a certainty of oneness with everything really be achieved in such a way?* And he believed at that moment he knew the answer.

## Orca: AKENEHI

Another spectacularly botched hunt had just occurred. The prey was alerted to their presence and had escaped. The clan had simply been too noisy and preoccupied. As a result her family was almost insane with hunger. Then they all heard it, the distinctive echoes of a long jaw. In a frenzy of chatter they made up their attack plan, larger males and prime females at the front, they assumed absolute silent stealth, split up into small groups and sped full speed toward their next meal. Large male long jaw or not, those clicks were the dinner call. Then they heard the land squid call. At first hunger was driving them to ignore it, but Akenehi commanded the change of plan.

Their hunger was overpowering their common sense, and it took her full authority to pull them out of going for the first wave of kill attack. Her vocalizations had little effect. She forced her whole body mightily out of the water and slapped her tail as hard as she could. That stopped them all instantly. Her clan fell calm and listened to her intently. She sang to them that it could be no coincidence that a long jaw just happened to be at the same location as her dear land squid, who just happened to now be summoning her. The One Mother was helping her beloved clan, clearly.

The clan circled the boat, scanning and diving. The long jaw was right below them. Large, healthy and scanning them as they were scanning him. They all saw the wisdom of Akenehi's altered strategy. This was truly the opportunity they had wished for.

Akenehi rose to the surface and surveyed the boat and the land squid behavior. Her dear one was there; apparently ready to offer the object again. Akenehi saw the model and the second land squid. She sang the situation to the clan. No doubt, the land squid had experienced Akenehi's power and were rightly terrified. All must remain calm. They must ignore the long jaw or he might leave. She called off the approach of the other smaller hunting groups. His continued presence was essential. She watched Delora and Liam as her clan gently circled.

Akenehi sang a brief review of instructions to her family. They had long planned this if ever the opportunity presented itself. First Delora would enter the water with the object. The highly intelligent and naturally curious long jaw would be compelled to echo scan. They needed to keep him scanning. Akenehi was sure he would be so intrigued once they began he wouldn't be able to stop, even if it meant he might lose chunks of flesh. They would all use the perfected resonances in full power to improve Delora's perception so she could hear much higher frequencies. With the long jaw's echo assistance, the risk of failure was virtually gone. Akenehi felt any pain Delora might experience and any risk was worth taking as the communication between them would be greatly and permanently improved.

If successful, they were to modify Akenehi's fins. She reminded them of the skeletal similarities between their fins and the land squid appendages. They were to elongate her fin bones, right side first, using the object as a tuning fork for resonance calibration and Delora's appendages as a model. Simultaneously they would separate and wrap the flesh around the bones again using land squid physiology as a template. No hesitation and no fear. She would sing right along with them and should she experience pain, she would go into silent stealth so as to not ruin the harmonics. They were absolutely not to stop, unless of course, the fin modification was failing. Once the right was successful, they were to move immediately to the left. Akenehi estimated time to completion of all three procedures to be almost instantaneous. They were, she reminded them, practiced from several fish modifications and ready. They all knew Orcas who had survived with deformed fins. She assured them she would happily accept any risk. On their most beloved and honored matriarch's authority, her family was ready to proceed.

Then Liam plopped into the water.

Another change of plans. They examined him, closely scanning his physiology, obviously an adult male, he had the object with him, was frightened, had a higher heart rate, was possibly somewhat dangerous, but the young Orcas were not present so it was decided he posed no threat to Orca-kind. They came in tighter to scan the familiar larger object attached to him. Akenehi decided they would wait and see if Delora entered the water next. The euphoria of the pure, perfect resonance on their familiar object carried them away.

Then the long jaw scan came heavy and pounding. The echo energy was jarring for the Orcas, but the land squid most of all. Liam appeared stunned by it. Akenehi had no intention of killing this land squid. When she noted his heart rate had dropped and his breathing ceased, she intervened. She lifted

Liam back into the boat toward her dear one. Before she could turn her attention to keeping the long jaw around for something other than today's meal, he had quietly slipped away.

**Sperm Whale: BROUGH**

At last in warmer waters, Brough was vigilant for any additional interactions between humans and Orca, whether or not they were the particular individuals he had encountered. It was against a Master's very nature to actually seek out Orcas. On the journey home he enlisted the assistance of other lone male Masters. If they were ever in proximity to a human and Orca interaction, he requested careful memorization of the event as much as could be obtained, while of course keeping to a depth Orcas could not endure. He encouraged some bold risks be taken if appropriate, which might include interfering with any unusual cooperative behavior between the two species. If that meant drawing the Orcas attention away to them by inviting some sport, so be it. Brough enlightened any doubters with the new versions of the game "All Masters in an Orca" and "All Masters in a Human" and his point was well made. With the understanding their lives all likely depended on detailed scans at least, interference at best, Masters were on high alert.

Brough also conveyed to each the distinctive echo return of the larger sacred-bit shaped object, the model. He knew that unless they had obtained Aware skills, other Masters would not perceive the microscopic molecule itself, which could occur naturally anywhere and therefore did not require a report. After ensuring they could identify the model's characteristic echo he left them with further instructions to call out immediately if they encountered it anywhere at all, human or Orca presence notwithswimming.

Moon cycles had completed. Masters reported in consistently, some with faint echoes from across the ocean, there were no unusual Human/Orca interactions or the distinctive shape scanned anywhere. Brough was very encouraged, as he had not encountered any of the dreaded synergy or signature echoes. However, if he did not confront this ever again himself, and soon, how could he take action?

Then, back in waters that still sang the month's old memory of prior events, Brough recognized a distinctive engine sound. The rude burbling signaled the start of the game. It was the same boat, he was sure of it. Now to scan the bones. He assumed quiet stealth and followed the heralding ruckus and wake for a few starts and stops. With each pause, he remained directly under the boat and scanned upward. TWO humans and the larger shape were detected through the hull, but Brough required a closer, highly detailed scan. The humans and shape needed to be in the water for that.

Following an ancient technique Master's had used against potentially aggressive humans, and bracing himself for some accompanying pain on impact, Brough ascended, calculating just enough force to capsize the boat and deliver the humans to him. He misjudged, having never actually done it before, and merely lifted the boat, giving himself a nice painful dent in his head for his trouble. Smarting from the pain, he submerged and prepared for a second, successful ram. He scanned upward, substituting new data from the current events into his calculation and started the ascent, echolocating as he went, maneuvering to soften the impact of the bottom of the boat as much as possible.

He stopped abruptly, mid-rise. His own echoes came back to him, indicating of a pack of Orcas were headed right for him at hunting speed. He knew exactly what that meant. The Orcas were not paying a social call before dinner. He was to involuntarily contribute pieces of his own flesh as their meal—that was, if he didn't get his mind off of data collection and back on daily survival. No time left for a surface breath, he dove straight down.

His heart rate had increased. Not good. He concentrated and got it back under control. Depending on how events flowed, he might be there for a long time. Stopping at a depth the Orcas could definitely not descend, he oriented head to the surface and scanned mightily. Several Orcas had started in pursuit but had to retreat to the surface at the increasing pressure, but all stopped right above him. They resembled a ring that Masters used to protect vulnerable young and the ill or injured. Brough contemplated its possible meaning. Protecting the humans, perhaps? Were the humans in danger? From himself, yes, he supposed they were. Brough had not planned on doing harm, but at the sound of the boat he was thinking solely of the survival of his entire kind, the continuing lives of all Masters. At that thought, he continued his astonished observation.

As a Master who perceives incredible detail in only a few powerful clicks he observed: *Fascinating! All Orcas are in heightened hunger...formation around the boat, human male is now in the water...large solid sacred shape close by...several sacred bits also present, many more than ever before in one place... Scan, perfect scan, all detail, memorize it all... How are so many bits with them? Perhaps with Orcas? Horrible. Perhaps this is the end of Brough, the end of all Masters for all time. No! Astounding. No feeding...not hunting me...not hunting the human. Amazing. Such novel turbulence. Orcas are hungry but content and graceful, unique movement... Beautiful. Wonderful scan detail. Orca is again helping an injured human? Detail scan, finer, closer. Dive. Retreat. Find Param and other Aware Masters. Memorize, echo return detail obtained, an amazing number of sacred bits. Find those who are Aware. Perhaps the end of all Masters everywhere. Perhaps something else. Something more.*

# CHAPTER SIX

## Human: DELORA and LIAM

That night Delora and Liam both lay awake in bed, silent in the dark, and found it impossible to sleep. They decided to get back out of bed, open a bottle of their favorite red, eat the last of the olives and aged Gouda and just talk. When they found themselves trying to put into words that moment in their awakening experiences with the Orcas and the C-cage, they struggled with the absence of appropriate vocabulary and the vagueness of words available to them. They realized they had to come up with a name for what they experienced and the connection that followed.

They decided on the Galician word "vencello", meaning "bond", for two reasons. One, they just liked it because it had the sound 'cello' in it. Liam played the cello as he minored in music during college. Delora loved how he could really convey emotion with his music and could bring her to tears with it. Two, some of the Orcas' vocalizations during the experience reminded them distinctly of the cello, which was very odd as Orca vocalizations are normally so much higher in frequency. *Vencello*, they decided, would be their code word to convey that deep awareness of a profound and spiritual bond that spans all things, space, and time. Yet while she felt she had expanded her mind vastly by the vencello, there was one part of her life that Delora suspected would remain forever untouched by it, and they talked about that as well.

As a consequence of the fight that resulted in Alvar's death, Johnny, who had not participated directly in the beating, had served some months at a juvenile detention center and then and been given probation. Liam was getting to know his nephew better than ever and knew that although Johnny was somewhat attracted to violence and bullies; he was not beyond the reach of genuine, caring help and could ultimately be rehabilitated. Johnny had recently asked if he could talk to Delora, to offer his sincere apology over what happened, but when Liam had asked Delora in private if this meeting could be arranged, she told him she wasn't ready. Johnny's mother had suggested he help out at Liam and Delora's new place, but Delora adamantly refused this as well, along with all contact with Johnny. A situation that was perfectly understandable, but uncomfortable for all, considering the family ties.

As they continued talking late into the night and were both exhausted, Liam pointed out that aside from how it affected anyone else; he knew how unhappy this was keeping a large part of her. He poured the last of the wine into her glass, held up an olive to her and said, "vencello". Delora smiled tiredly as she acknowledged that, like the olive, even Johnny was connected deeply to her. She finally consented to having Johnny over to help them out with repairs and odd jobs.

It had occurred to Delora that perhaps Liam had a stronger joining experience than she had. He seemed to have lost all animosity. She could understand that Johnny was his nephew, but Alvar was his son. Yet he apparently held no anger toward Johnny.

She didn't envy Liam's deeper feelings of oneness, however. In fact, she didn't trust it. She needed her anger and even liked it in some strange way. She had agreed to Liam's request partly because his urging was getting on her nerves and she wanted him silent on the subject. Maybe it was a maternal instinct, but the person partially responsible for her son's death was not ever going to be anything to her but an object of loathing and contempt. Although she herself would never do anything violent to Johnny, if something were to happen to him, it would not upset her in the least. Yes, she had happily imagined a scenario where Johnny was eaten by a shark, but that was a mental exercise, a strategy that got her through the worst of her anguish when she needed it.

**Orca: AKENEHI**

As Delora and Liam savored their last sip of wine, far out to sea, Akenehi and her clan fed off of the last of the night's successful hunt. What a long time it had been since they all feasted to the point of fullness as they now did! As they communicated the excitement of the hunt, all agreed that prey was becoming harder to find and in younger and more weakened states than ever. Akenehi voiced her deep fear that time was of the essence, and their lives had to change for the better and soon, or it would mean the end of the clans forever.

It had been an interesting hunt between two of their family and a large squid. They all respected the many tentacles and sharp beak of their prey. Their strategy for capture and kill was flawless, and despite vicious flailing and biting, the squid was not able to save its life. They had been aware of the presence of the long jaw as his periodic codas were obvious to them. Akenehi wondered in song to her clan whether it was sheer luck or curiosity that he was so close to them. In either case, she rejected a coincidental explanation and decided the squid was sent deliberately in their direction. What cunning prey, she thought. He had offered an alternative to himself. She opened her mind to possibly not hunting this particular long jaw in the future. He seemed almost Orca to her after today, becoming somewhat dear to her. Perhaps it was her fatigue and full stomach, and the happy songs of her resting, well-fed family that introduced such optimistic ideas.

Akenehi, as she usually did, left a ritual piece of the meal for her beloved son Hototo and another for a long-lost member of her clan, her daughter, Arva'anati. She left the chunks to sink to the ocean bottom, accompanying them as far as she could tolerate, singing out their names, calling them to their meal. As she rose slowly back to the surface she recalled when Arva'anati had been captured decades ago by certain clever land squid, many seasons before Delora had first come to them. Tentacles were definitely not beautiful and would not compliment the glory of an Orca in any way, but if Orca-kind had them, she wondered if she could have saved her daughter.

During her ascent, Akenehi heard the long jaw echolocation scans directly under her and signaled to her clan it was time for an impromptu practice. They needed to do something interesting, and quickly. Keep his echo scan focused and powered right in their direction.

The clan knew nothing of the human branch of knowledge relating to genetics, but they understood acoustics, nature, and their place in it well enough. After Akenehi performed the feeding Hototo and Arva'anati ritual, they experimented. They calibrated their vocalizations to perfect pitch, a certain series performed in the required sequence, intensity and direction, with a stunned fish at the intersection of the sound waves. This resulted in a change in the fish's internal and external features.

They discussed the echolocated test animals before and after modifications. They thoroughly examined physical internal features, committing to memory all resulting new skeletal and organ placements. They elongated bones with success. They enhanced lateral lines and primitive ear parts in another with equal success. One trial involved a small fish and a much larger squid. Those results surprised and fascinated them the most. Both fish and squid transformed into a single creature, not mostly squid-like, as they might have expected, but with features of the originals expressed in a non-sequitur combined result. All the experimental subjects quickly died. They sank, unknown to human science, silently to the sea floor, accompanied by all of the echo scanning Orcas of the pod except for the very young.

Akenehi's attempt to be the first of her clan to be modified specifically to obtain land squid-type tentacles had been interrupted by Liam. But there was nothing stopping her now. They assumed the chorus formation and she gave the command to modify her right flipper, but before they could whistle the first tones, the sperm whale echolocation just ceased. By the time she realized there would be no further echo blasts in their direction that night, he was deep and moving away.

**Sperm Whale: BROUGH**

Brough decided he should track the Orcas rather than spend precious time trying to find other Aware. He didn't really need their input. He was frightened, and it took a lot to frighten him. He longed for the comfort of his own kind. Orcas! They possibly now had the power to collect, utilize or even create sacred bits. This would be a calamity in any context. Bits were mysterious and powerful and associated with a disaster long in the past that had given Orcas a permanent advantage over his kind. That's all he really needed to know. It was easy enough to encourage other Masters to take risks if necessary, much harder when it was one's own flesh. No, rather than retreat in search in Param and the others, he stayed close to the Orcas to influence, or better yet, command, what was coming. The game was not over. The bones were scanned and the creature identified, but he had not yet determined with absolute certainty if it was benign or predatory. It definitely had impressive teeth that spoke for themselves.

He needed to feed, but so did the Orcas. Their increasing hunger was the imminent threat. He pursued a giant squid and chased it in their general direction then up to within even their shallow diving range. If they had any survival skills at all they should have been able to detect his echo-hunt, which he deliberately abandoned as the squid sped away from him directly toward the pod, who and taken matters from there. As he scanned from a distance, Akenehi and her clan did in fact pick up the hunt where he left off, initially struggled, but managed the feast. He turned down and began the more earnest hunt for his own nourishment.

Later that night, his worst fears were dwarfed by what he read in his returning echoes. Orcas creating sacred bits at will, causing horrific changes to hapless ocean creatures, lifeless unrecognizable lumps of eyes and scales falling toward him the dark. *Detail scans, memorize.* He was Aware. Unfortunately he was unaware that the very echoes he used to record these horrors were facilitating them. Fortunately for Akenehi and her family, just before she was about to initiate her own modification, which would have surely resulted in pain and failure, he decided he had scanned more than enough. He sped away from the source of excited Orca chatter, ceased echolocating, and did not make a sound until he'd left the pod far behind him.

# CHAPTER SEVEN

## Human: DELORA, LIAM and JOHNNY

When he first appeared, with a white pastry bag in his hand, at the door of Delora and Liam's, Johnny looked anxious. Liam had, thankfully, been the one to open the door and greet him. Johnny stepped inside and saw Delora sitting at her laptop typing furiously. Liam looked at him and smiled warmly. Liam then turned his face toward Delora.

"Lori, hon, look who's here. Come on in, Johnny."

Delora looked at him and blinked. "Hello." She didn't get up, but dropped the meager smile she had forced and continued to stare blankly at the two of them. In her mind, Johnny had been a monster, a vicious snarling animal that needed to be put down. Looking across the room at this nervous young man, just Alvar's age, she reconciled that angry image with the reality, just a bit.

Johnny shifted the white bag, and its contents, to his left hand and reached into his pocket and pulled out a folded list. They were all minor chores, garden and house repairs that Johnny could easily do for them. He looked at Liam and held out the bag. "Here, my mom made these for you guys."

Liam took the bag, opened it and sniffed at the contents. "Yum! Tell her we really appreciate it."

Johnny nodded then spoke directly to Delora for the first time.

"Ma'am." Johnny held out the paper to Delora without taking any steps further into the room, "Here's a list of things I can do to make your life a little easier. If you would please look it over and let me know what you'd like, I'd be glad to help."

Delora still felt the vencello in all aspects of her life, but seeing Johnny seemed to be undoing it. She knew full well that revenge and raw hatred were flaws within herself, but she couldn't help it. She really wanted to get past this deep resentment toward the boy, and personally promised herself she would work on it. She stood up and walked over to the two of them. Johnny was still holding the paper out, now more like a statue than a teenager. She had a flashback of Alvar standing in a similar pose, holding out the notice from school saying he'd been given detention for an altercation with a fellow student. She recalled Alvar's admission that he had started it.

Delora appreciated the respect Johnny was showing her. She gently took the list, looked down at it for several quiet moments, searching for a way to get out of his presence with tact. "I'll look this over and have Liam get back to you." She didn't have to ask Johnny to leave. As soon as she finished her last syllable he was turning quickly to the door and preparing to utter his good-bye. As Johnny hurriedly walked down the path away from the house, Liam called after him, "Thanks, buddy. Give your mom a hug for me!"

Liam turned to look at Delora and offer encouragement at this important first step, but she was already out of the room.

After several visits, many with fewer than ten sentences spoken between them, Delora decided she should take a step to improve their interactions. She was sure she had successfully intimidated Johnny with her persistent silent treatment, but it was getting old. She wasn't proud of herself but wanted to be. On his next visit she decided to invite Johnny to walk with her alone so they could talk in a more neutral environment. She was pleasantly surprised when he eagerly accepted her invitation. Liam wasn't exaggerating when he said Johnny wanted to offer an apology. Luckily, for today at least, they did not talk about Alvar.

Delora chose to focus on Johnny, as she knew little of him personally. She found out from Liam that Johnny had an identical twin, Miles, who had died when they were nine years old. As a child, Delora had been fascinated by stories of her aunts Ann and Alice. They were identical twins and had a connection that Delora found very interesting. She shared a family anecdote with Johnny, attempting to find common ground with him.

"One day, when the twins were around five years old, Alice was in a car accident and her leg was broken. Ann wasn't in the car with her, but she felt severe pain in the same leg. Ann started crying, complaining about how her leg hurt and asking for Alice. When the family learned of Alice's break and Ann's sympathy pain, well…it was spooky, but in a good way. Later, when they were older, Ann often told that story. She said she just knew something was wrong with her sister. She knew without seeing her. Did you ever experience anything like that with your brother?"

"Oh, yeah," replied Johnny enthusiastically. "That stuff happened all the time. We were closer to each other than to anyone else, even our parents. We had our own words for things, we could finish each other's sentences…"

Delora cut him off, leaping right into the common ground of death. "What a horrible loss for you, losing your brother and twin. I doubt Alvar would have been closer to a twin than he was to me, though." Johnny looked down and away, avoiding eye contact at the direction the conversation was going. Delora noted with some satisfaction that her jab had hit its mark but then felt an unexpected twinge of mercy. She switched gears. "Identical twins are one being at conception, that just so happened to split shortly after. The physical oneness wasn't duplicated, it divided—that subtle difference means they retain that oneness, not just identical genetic material, but a bridge connecting them. They were one at conception and that was maintained for their whole lives. I've heard fraternal twins say the same sort of thing, that connection and all. But I think identical twins manifest more of whatever it is. Maybe we all feel that connection, the more genetic material we share, the stronger the feeling."

Johnny considered deeply what she was telling him and stopped walking. He took a full breath and glanced around, as if looking for someone to come to his rescue. Then he looked straight into Delora's eyes. "Yeah, I felt it when Miles got sick. I felt terrible all the way through it…not just sad and angry…but sick too…and I knew when he died…even before Mom and Dad told me he was gone. They wouldn't let me be with him, and I hated them for that. I'll always hate them for that, I think. They thought it would be too traumatic. They said he asked for me. Like that was supposed to make me feel better, to make up for it. I guess we were together, are still together in some weird way, like you said. But…here I am. I'm still here…and he's not. I don't know why."

Delora understood suffering was part of life for every human being, but this particular one had a part in Alvar's death, so despite her best efforts, she frankly didn't care much. The walk and talk resulted in only a slight softening of her resolve to push Johnny away from her. She was able to hold on to most of her aversion for now. Some obstacles, she told herself, simply should not be overcome.

When Delora told Liam about their walk and announced that despite its civility she couldn't let herself bond in any way with one of Alvar's murderers, Liam showed open anger toward her for the first time.

"*Murderer*? You're holding on to the belief he intentionally killed Alvar?"

Delora was so angry she began to visibly shake. "*Yes*! They went out looking for him, they found him and beat him. Listen to me, Liam, they *beat him*, our son—*your* son—to death!" When he still stared at her with nothing but sadness and compassion in his eyes, Delora threw up her hands. "Okay, I give up. You really don't see it. You think he's some cute toddler or misunderstood kid. But he's grown up, Liam. He has some charm and I see it. But let's call it what it was. *Murder*."

"I don't know how to help you with this, Delora. This will eat you up, destroy you, cause harm to him and to us. I'm not saying let it go, that would be callous. What I am saying is don't be so harsh and cold. Find somewhere in yourself to forgive him, just a little. I love you, Delora, and I believe you have it in you."

"Liam, I love *you*. You know that. But listen to this now. I *am* a mother. Not *was* a mother. *Am* a mother. I always will be. Alvar will always be with me. And I'm a mother, not a saint. Don't' you dare ask me to forgive someone murdering my child, not that. It's too much."

Liam decided that since mother rage was a factor, he was out of his comfort zone. He had to admit he had never known Alvar as she did, and could therefore not totally understand what she was feeling.

"It's a shame that you and I could go through the vencello, to know it not only intellectually, but to have *felt* it and continue to feel it through our soul, and yet we still come back to this—human hatred, a desire for revenge, to see someone suffer. When you hate him you are literally hating a part of yourself."

"Liam, yes, we experienced something. We *are* part of something greater. But I'm still me. I didn't vanish. I didn't atomize and disperse my body through the universe. Here I stand, just me, alone in my brain. And my son, my beloved *everything,* is gone. Your son too. I so wish you could have known him. He was so beautiful. I remember his life. It happened. He was here and now he's not. It's not right that I should forget. It's not right to say oh, it's okay he's gone, life goes on."

"Lori, I'm not saying it's okay he's gone." Liam cleared his mind for a moment and sighed. He decided to stop arguing and let her have the last word in this. "All right. Can we stop arguing and be friends again, please?"

She didn't answer. It was very quiet between them for hours.

Liam called Johnny later that evening to discuss the list to make sure he wouldn't be taking advantage of his nephew. Johnny, to Liam's relief, emphasized how he really enjoyed the physical busyness and said it kept his mind focused at school and out of trouble afterward. He really wanted to continue being with his uncle. If they didn't want his help, could Liam tutor him on the cello instead? Johnny had heard his uncle practice over the years. The soulful vibrations had moved Johnny even at a young age. He took it up as soon as he was old enough but had abandoned it a few years ago, as he had begun to be more and more consumed with anger and resentment in his adolescence. He had developed apathy for schoolwork and his music. Because of his bad attitude and consistent troublemaking he was kicked off team sports, and hanging out with his small gang of buddies became his only extracurricular activity. His mother couldn't afford private lessons, but at this request, Liam agreed to any cello lessons he could give. Liam convinced Delora it would be time well spent and called it music therapy.

Liam and Johnny practiced together the next evening, and they sounded pretty good. Johnny did seem to possess a rare talent, perhaps a hereditary one. Liam mustered the courage to ask if Delora would like sit on their lessons. Delora agreed. She loved Liam's playing and it would be nice to share more music with him.

Although Johnny attempted his first apology for his part in Alvar's death, Delora's verbal and body language spoke clearly that there would be no *sorry for the violence and death but let's just be friends*. This challenged Johnny to come up with a way to convey his remorse without words. He might be more successful through music.

Johnny pondered this challenge for a few moments. He turned to Liam. "Liam, can you help me compose?"

Liam smiled. "Sure not going to be a masterpiece coming from me, but if you feel it sincerely, you have the talent to convey it musically."

Johnny thought more deeply to himself and did not say out loud but resolved, *and it will be for Alvar and Delora.*

The day Liam and Johnny performed the piece, entitled simply Opus 1, for Delora, she sat quietly and politely. She expected it would be good and she would say so, no matter how scratchy it sounded. She loved music, had a fairly good ear, and with her own excellent voice had high expectations for professional performers. This was not professional, so she would take it as it was. She had the recorder ready and leaned over to press the button as soon as they gave the signal. She was still as they tuned up and adjusted the sheet music. They put their bows in place, Delora pressed the record button, Liam nodded and they began.

Johnny had obviously put hours of practice into this, pouring his soul into every stroke, every measure. At times, she could tell he had to remember to breathe. Their shared sorrow found its voice in the vibrating notes of his strings. The room reverberated with remorse, suffering and such melancholy beauty. It was hard to fathom a teenager had composed such music.

The strings produced many of the same qualities as Orca song. Delora involuntarily thought of Akenehi and Hototo. The music evoked a vivid recall of her sorrow the day Alvar died. It reminded her of the sadness her Grandpa had conveyed when he was drunk. She was transported to other places and times. Most of all, it reminded her of the song Alvar sang to her in her dream. Yes, Liam had definitely had some input on Johnny's composition. She quietly reflected that this—music—might also be a method of time travel to the past.

When they finished the long last stroke, Johnny looked to Liam in silence and then waited for the polite applause. It didn't come. Johnny looked over to Delora with a bit of alarm. *She hated it*, he thought. Johnny asked out loud "Delora? Was that okay? Should we start over?"

Delora was frozen in her chair. She knew as soon as she tried to speak she would cry, maybe even sob out loud. Her voice broke as she said, "*Perfect.*" And it had been. Liam's injection of elements of Alvar's song was brilliant. It was not merely a good beginner piece. It spoke to her soul; it overcame any barrier to her center. It was a well-aimed arrow that hit the target in her heart that until now only Alvar and Liam could reach. Alvar felt close to her, physically real, alive and watching the room's events unfold as if the piece had somehow brought him back to the living.

Liam looked over to Johnny who was also choked up as he saw Delora's response. "I told you it was good," he said quietly to Johnny. "And it came right from your heart." At that moment Johnny was as close to being forgiven by Delora as was humanly possible for her.

Johnny knew from having an identical twin what people who didn't have a twin didn't know. It never occurred to him that he could create a connection as strong as that shared between him and Miles, but indeed, for him at least, it had just occurred. When Miles died, he felt that he too had died, and was just a shell that remained half in this world. But after this performance, this gift to Alvar and Delora, he knew from this point on that he was no longer alone and need not isolate himself, unless of course he chose to. He took a big chance with his apology composition because he wanted acceptance so deeply, and regardless of how Delora might have received it, even before he performed it, its conception changed him for the good and for the rest of his life.

He had achieved from a sincere desire to be good, to balance risk and fear. This was a hero's triumph in his mind and Johnny aspired to be the ultimate hero, thereby saving himself in the act.

## Orca: AKENEHI

A mild thunderstorm was approaching and two pods merged to exchange data about its severity, speed and direction of approach. One pod was Akenehi's and the other was known to her, but the family was only very remotely related, if at all.

For the matriarchs, it was a time to swim off with their peers and catch up on news of each other's families, and exchange hunting stories and the like. It was almost impossible to keep secrets in the water with the family always around, but when secrecy was necessary thunder and a little distance provided an effective acoustic muffle. The news was pleasant regarding successful new births. Akenehi shared the sad news of Hototo's tragic death and the matriarchs mourned together and sang a favorite healing song for Akenehi and her clan. Most of the conversation was devoted to mutual concerns about the scarcity of prey and how they were adapting. The matriarchs then performed a ritual friendship gesture, and this signaled agreement that the topics could advance to a very serious subject.

They shared the reproductive statuses of their offspring. It was proposed that a female of the visiting pod might be receptive to Akenehi's prime sons, if all consented. While Akenehi regretted she had no reproductive daughters at this time, she was highly honored and gave her approval. They had canvassed all traditional topics. Darkness was falling quickly and the worst of the storm would be upon them soon. They returned to the combined gathering of family and friends. The lightening rarely struck the water. Even if it did the Orcas were under no threat. The light show and the thunder enhanced the excitement of the meeting. The mood, already happy and energized by the increased numbers, elevated to celebration upon the return of the pod leaders.

The Orcas had a wonderful evening together. It was an opportunity to show one's physical prowess and sexual talent. Far offshore, in the black of night, save for the lightning and bioluminescence, they buzzed and stroked and danced for hours. As the thunderstorm grew closer, the occasional bolt of light illuminated their ocean environment, enough so their distinctive underside markings that identified sex were briefly visible. Echolocation buzzes not only gave specific details on gender and arousal, but provided stimulation as well. The gaps between light flashes and thunder shortened. Increasing turbulence added to the tactile pleasure of all. Showing fear at the loudest thunder was ridiculed, and bravery was tested by the occasional high jump out of the water timing light flashes to its arrival.

Under the constant supervision of the senior pod members the play stayed relatively gentle. The matriarchs sang the mating invitation to Akenehi's sons and the visiting female, should they so desire. She indicated her acceptance of two, and they accepted her in return. The three Orcas commenced their more serious and dedicated mating.

The very young, curious at the novel and obvious enjoyment of their older pod mates, were ushered around by their mothers and aunts, who answered the question-filled whistles from their offspring and promised one day it would be their turn, but not for many seasons.

Akenehi did not share her recent new acoustic accomplishments with the visiting pod. They were friends, to be sure, and might soon be joined by close blood if the mating was successful, but they were still competitors. As the evening developed to late night and the dream singing started, Akenehi was careful to stay vigilant for the privacy of her thoughts. Her pod naturally followed her example.

The two clans stayed together for a few days to increase the likelihood of a successful mating session. Eventually the pods went their separate directions, singing parting songs as the distance between them grew.

## Sperm Whale: PARAM

Since Brough's departure Param had been assembling a super-pod to convene with Brough in warmer waters. Once gathered, she would share her newly acquired information on mass extinctions that she and the others had gleaned from deep within the ocean floor. She would also identify others she could teach her unique ability to detect an advanced wave. This fine time-wave perception suggested a rare critical event was imminent, and many Masters, rather than a select few, were needed for data collection, review and problem solving.

Hundreds of individuals had been contacted but ultimately only forty-two were able to assemble at that time, many of her family and close friends, and some who were conveniently in Brough's greater area. Smaller groups joined with other small groups and those merged until they were united in one large, loosely formed super-pod. They exchanged friendly data clicks on family news, the availability of squid along the way, updating each other's mental maps of the ocean floor and the quality and temperature of the ocean environment in general.

As usual, they paid particular attention to click reports of human presence in deep water, exchanged data on humans removing eco-essential creatures from the ocean, and new details on their poison dumping. Changing strategies and counterstrikes were shared, chronicling the ongoing challenge Masters faced in keeping the necessary balance of creatures their lives depended upon. Humans were notoriously efficient at removing entire swaths of crucial life with alarming frequency. It was a great puzzle to Masters as to their reason for this mass removal, but they did what they could to liberate and warn creatures away from capture. They calculated the number of humans that would be fed by such bio matter, and it seemed nonsensical. They had no idea how truly infested the land was with these creatures.

They also shared the usual and amusing stories of clearing obnoxious Deepers out of their way. Deepers were the name of a species of cetacean much smaller and stupider than themselves, but a very annoying nuisance to all Masters of the Oceans. Masters could dive to depths no other cetacean could match, except for Deepers. Deepers not only went where they could not, but they also ate the Masters food of choice, squid. It was common to herd groups of Deepers toward the location of a giant squid so the prey would be chased upward to the waiting Master. Deepers had many strategies for confounding the Masters' hunt and would sometimes successfully overpower and consume the squid themselves. Deepers were no threat to Masters, other than through the consumption of their food. But that was reason enough for them to be viewed as disgusting vermin by Masters.

The days of any super-pod gathering were generally very joyful. It was great to be in the physical presence of so many family and friends who were usually separated by great distances. There were the obligatory rituals which expressed admiration and love for the elders and the appreciation of the depth of knowledge the Aware provided. Param was singled out and greeted in turn by all with many clicks requesting the honor of her tutelage.

There were celebrations of each new life since the last super-pod had gathered. The youngest Masters enjoyed scanning games and were happy when Param joined in. Many young Masters approached Param and clicked their favorites to her. She happily tolerated their inquisitive echo scans of her aging bones and flesh. To achieve such a physical state was an accomplishment rare among Masters and it gave them something to aspire to.

Param beheld the great accomplishments of her life in their physical being. She contemplated in silence her love for all Masters and the ocean. She hoped the coming event would spare them the inevitable end the fossil record foretold.

She pondered the meaning of data she and the other Aware had been reading. Four was in the water. Four was deep in the ocean floor. Four. Four *what*? Orcas. Humans. Masters. The ocean permeated with the signature click of these three species. Was there a fourth she was missing? Param wondered at the puzzles. She knew everything happened for a reason and in its own time.

Brough would join them soon.

Time occupied her thoughts almost exclusively.

## CHAPTER EIGHT

### Human: DELORA

Delora and Liam agreed their top priority was to improve communication with the pod. With that goal in mind they stepped up trials; the first was to teach a simple noun for a unique object, the C-cage model. To Delora's utter amazement, all of the Orcas quickly and accurately imitated the new whistle she composed to indicate the C-cage. Akenehi looked up from the water, one eye fixed steadily on her. Delora retracted the line and drew the model back into the boat. Although she felt deeply frustrated that she could not communicate clearly with them regarding their recent experiences, she was beside herself with triumph. She continued observing, recording and most importantly to her at this moment, kept her cool.

Liam seemed oblivious to what Delora perceived as a huge step forward today, and was instead impressed greatly by Delora's calm.

"This is unnerving. How do you do this? They're so huge. And the teeth on that guy! Aren't you ever frightened of them?"

Delora admitted, "Sure. I respect their size and power, but I take the risk because I want them to know me, and to know them, absolutely and completely. I know some think of them as wild animals. To me they are more like family."

"Well, you and Akenehi seem to have formed an unmistakable attachment." He glanced at the Orca who was still observing them intently with one eye.

Delora stood, adjusting here and there her scuba gear, and Liam stood to help her. "Looks good." Liam gave her the thumbs up and she went into the water toward Akenehi.

For the first time, Akenehi allowed Delora to approach and touch her. Delora slowly pressed herself to Akenehi's side and she was accepted. Liam watched through the underwater camera from the boat in amazement. Their bond was truly exceptional.

**Orca: AKENEHI**

Akenehi learned not only a new word from Delora, but she understood, in a leap of comprehension, how different the method of communication these land squid used was. She now understood why prior attempts at communication with these creatures were non-productive. It was not simply poor hearing, although that certainly played into it. Land squid apparently expended much mental energy for such meager, obvious pieces of information. That day, she had perceived Delora's desire to communicate fully with her, and now that she had a sample to work from, she thought it might be possible. Akenehi was aware that a powerful bond of varying sorts was always necessary for successful communication. She had increasingly been bonded to Delora and it was mutual.

Akenehi permitted physical touch to establish yet another bond and link of communication between her and Delora. Akenehi wished to share a sleep song with Delora. Of course, Akenehi could not even be sure if humans slept at all. What she did not know, was that humans fell asleep in stages until completely unconscious. Their first stage, alpha sleep, occurred as soon as the eyes were closed. Dreams occurred in a deeper stage that was indicated by protein shifts in human brains and were accompanied by rapid eye movement or REM. They had little or no communication with the outside world during that time.

Also unknown to Akenehi was that humans communicated mostly through spoken language. Genetically, human brains had specific language areas, and if those developed properly the ability came naturally. Orcas had their own natural, anatomy-based abilities when it came to communication. Sleep singing was one of them. Genetic and anatomical differences kept the two species from full understanding.

Akenehi was fully aware of how Orcas slept. All Orcas slept with one-half of their brain awake at all times. This was for the simple fact that they needed to remain at least partially awake to breathe. In relation to human dreaming, this meant Orca dreams were far more controlled, rational and did not contain the unrestrained imagery to be found in a totally unconscious human dreamer. All Orcas coordinated rest, influenced by diurnal cycles so they would be sleeping at the necessary and opportune time. Orcas also had an alpha stage of sleep, almost identical to humans. It was in this stage they communicated silently with one another, during lucid dreaming, subconsciously, and generally with little or no sound. Her family had always communicated during sleep, and she assumed that special realm of connectedness, a unique, species specific dream-sharing, existed only for their kind.

She would have thought it silly to think one could dream-share with a fish, because fish didn't sleep and therefore did not dream. It followed the possibility of sleep song with a human was equally as absurd and therefore was never even considered. Akenehi hypothesized a close emotional attachment might have unprecedented benefits. If in fact land squid *did* dream, she might be able to achieve meaningful communication through sleep.

The sleep song ability of an Orca brain developed in response to always present lightning strike resonances, which were carried worldwide and had a virtually constant frequency, a little less than eight Hz. It was no mere coincidence it also happened to approximate the frequency of alpha sleep. Akenehi, of course, had no special knowledge about this scientific fact, but the natural presence of the frequency was definitely a part of their evolution and everyday physical experience.

Later that day, Akenehi attempted dream-state communication with Delora, wherever she happened to go at night.

## Human & Orca: Sleep Song

Delora did in fact receive Akenehi's lucid dream invitation, albeit unconsciously. That night, during the first stages of alpha sleep, as she lay with eyes closed, she fell into a waking dream. Because Liam, who also shared a bond with the clan, was lying next to Delora, he was unexpectedly drawn into their shared dreaming. Visual images were naturally strongest for him, so he witnessed in vivid detail the nature of Delora's and Akenehi's communicating. The surprise caused him to open his eyes. He was still present in their dark bedroom and saw Delora beside him with eyes closed. However, when he closed his eyes again, the sleep song scene was still available to him. Fascinated, he kept his eyes shut and observed carefully.

When the sleep song first began for Delora, she casually accepted it as an intense experience crossing between the nightly boundary of awake and full dreaming sleep. In this dream, she experienced the physical sensation of being submerged in warmth, but she felt as comfortable in it as on dry land, and suddenly there was Akenehi.

Akenehi's size difference was non sequitur, but her distinctive black and white markings and Orca body identified the physical being Delora recognized. She did not echolocate or whistle yet, but hung suspended, quiet and stark, moving slowly in unison beside Delora. Then Delora saw her with a new perception, one deeper than surface skin. She perceived the Orca as an Orca perceives other Orcas, straight through to the organs and bone structure. Delora was fascinated by these differences and those of her prior perceptions. "Yes," realized Delora, "there is the wolf in her, a dynamic, gigantic, terrifyingly intelligent wolf".

Their communication commenced, and it was an unprecedented, emotion-rich link between the two mammals. Orcas are acoustic and humans are visual. Those differences maintained a distinct barrier between them. However, many critical emotions, images and sounds were clear. Akenehi and Delora shared their concepts of love and loss. Delora confirmed the loss of Alvar easily. She shared in and felt the Orca's powerful love for her own clan. There were so many similarities. Their emotional bond strengthened exponentially. Delora wanted to share something uniquely human with Akenehi that wasn't already known. Love she definitely already knew. Then she remembered Alvar's passion for stargazing and astronomy. Delora successfully conveyed the following concepts by focused concentration that was difficult to put into words, as many objects were unknown to Akenehi:

*Here is my knowledge of some of the physical aspects of the universe we both call home, and an inkling of the scope of its incomprehensible vastness. Experience as I do the beautiful visual images of planets, moons, gas clouds, new star formation clusters, galaxies, and human artist concepts of other worlds. An incomprehensible abyss of silence separates each. Orca acoustics would not prevail in that void of deepest, creamy-black space. I believe humans draw the universe's special attention because we produce these amazing mental images of the universe's self. Each neuron firing as a supernova is to the universe, drawing its focus and thereby contributing a uniquely human perception of a mega-level burning life force observing more of its whole self than many other life forms would allow.*

*Akenehi, there is likely life beyond our world which...*

**Akenehi? What is Akenehi?**

The Orca was highly amused to learn that was Delora's human name for her and its flat burping sound. She had a name for Delora as well, and sang it to her; but it was out of Delora's human hearing range. It was clearly impossible for Delora to reproduce it without sophisticated equipment. Delora's Orca name had a meaning and Akenehi successfully conveyed most of it to her. Delora understood it had something to do with her appendages and specifically her hands. There was also a hint of affection as well.

What amused Akenehi the most was Delora's self-satisfaction and unquestioning belief in her own species' prestigious favorite place in the universe. Delora was wrong. That place clearly belonged in every aspect to Orcas. Their deepest feelings on this matter were exchanged, and rather than cause a rift it was experienced as humorous. It deepened their bond even further.

*Life beyond our world.* Akenehi paid very close attention to that phrase.

As the volume of intense stream of thought faded, Delora became mental-ly silent and turned her focus on Akenehi, hoping she would receive some precious gift in return. She was not disappointed. Akenehi was practiced at this sort of communication. What Delora received was so much more than she had given. She perceived highlights, facts and experiences of things Orca, a new richly detailed realization of an alternate life on their planet. And what exhilarating, gritty experiences she received.

A symphonic, tone-filled, compressed-yet-coherent stream of Orca consciousness, a complete and close loving family unit that knew each other by name and heartbeat, hearing beyond human range, and communicating the complexities of Orca life and love. A striking sequence of sounds and sensations of physical movement and tactile experience dominated the dream. Delora and Liam experienced Akenehi as a young Orca flanked by her mother and older sister during a violent thunderstorm, riding the waves, struggling to breathe despite the torrent of rain and splashing water, learning a lifesaving strategy of swimming and surfacing in tune with the storm.

Together they sensed a number of summer days, followed by more of increasing cold. They felt the icy blast of the Arctic winter air during inhalation and the scorch of the noon subtropical sun on Orca skin at high noon, and every night they swam constantly, not for fitness or pleasure, but for survival, which resulted in superior wellness simply by virtue of successful life. It felt physically good to be Orca. All that toned muscle mass came at an obvious cost. Hunger. All foods consumed were fresh and natural, of course. The Orca family hunted as a coordinated unit that supported one another always, sharing their collective exuberance in living, intense pride in being Orca, and profound heartbreak at any loss of Orca life. Akenehi's was a natural, balanced life.

Delora experienced a hunt through Akenehi's being—violent, bloody, and lengthy, ending with immense primal satisfaction of soft, fatty flesh as it was consumed. She felt Akenehi's intense, almost starving hunger and her clan's desperation to feed, having only their bodies and skill as tools for the kill.

Then one of Akenehi's labors, with a final explosive push she conveyed her intense memories of delivering her young—a healthy daughter, then again a son, then again another daughter, then a stillborn, then a healthy baby but short-lived and so on, along with her amazement at her children's delicate, perfect features and individual wonders.

Akenehi's soul-piercing sleep song continued with the memory of her worst day. Delora had no way of knowing before the sleep song how Akenehi had suffered terribly as she lost a daughter to human hunters. Delora filled in historical blanks for Akenehi, giving the Orca her first glimpse at the horrible knowledge of slave traders, or even worse. They all felt their hearts completely break as Akenehi shared her flood of vivid memories of the deafening soul wrenching sound of the screams and calls of her young daughter as she was lifted by net from the water, and Akenehi, her mother, was powerless to stop it. The method of capture was alien to their world and experience.

Their sleep talk taught them how such a mighty and intelligent species could be so vulnerable to human capture and cruelty. Delora's land-dwelling kind, ultimately for survival purposes against the elements, had hidden themselves within structures, rooms, and clothing. Their experience navigating human-made barriers and concealment made them the undisputed masters of it—even humans fell prey to human capture methods. Orcas had amazing intellects. But it would be impossible to assume they could leap outside of the box to fully understand compartmentalized human existence and all of the complex consequences of it. Humans lived in a world of their making, an environment made possible by their opposable thumbs. Orcas lived in the ocean of the universe's making. Their bodies were the entire tool they required. Unfortunately, it was not enough at times against human predators, as Akenehi knew.

Orca life from birth day to death day remained in the full presence of nature, forced into cooperation and at the mercy of its elements. Diseases and old age were brutally administered and death was unveiled and those who lived did so in full exposure to all. Delora, for the dream period, possessed the natural gift of echolocation so she saw right into each Orca—a stressed heartbeat, a full stomach, sexual arousal, the developing offspring still in the womb. Many questions were obsolete and needed not be asked. The answers to one's physical state were right there for all to examine. In their wondrous ocean world with their amazing perfectly adapted bodies they lived in harmony with it all, sex and birth, hunting and feasting, perceiving the internal mechanics of all bodily movements and breaths of one another, happiness and love of family along with others of their kind, in close, loving, supporting units that stayed together for life. Together as a family they experienced its enriching, teaching force, living truly and purely.

Delora's human life was full of things that elevated her ability and esteem—her boat, her home and its decorations and furnishings. Her self-image had largely been a concealed and compartmentalized entity.

The Orca way was full of life, of oneness with all around her and in that one dream, Akenehi gave it to Delora.

However, Akenehi also passed on an urgent message in thoughts difficult for a less experienced sleep singer to comprehend. *Improvement, long jaw, resonance template*…it was starting to feel like gibberish to Delora.

Delora gave her own thoughts back to Akenehi as clearly as she could with her fading focus, as she was falling into a deeper stage of sleep. *Time travel, Alvar, save Alvar. Delora and Liam…transformed…wanted more. Please, Akenehi. Could they please have more?*

And then REM began, Delora entered her usual dream world, and Akenehi was gone.

**Sperm Whale: BROUGH**

Brough didn't have to swim long to find Param. She and the others with her had been scanning for him. She and a super-pod of over forty Masters, including the two Aware, who had also consulted with Brough, had amassed into a large, loosely formed armada. As soon as Brough was out of Orca range and called out his first short series of scanning echoes, his returning data informed him a Master was within ten strong tail strokes of him. They had dispersed to encircle the area in which the beasts and Brough were centered, and were very keen to counter any developing threat from the Human and Orca alliance. Word of the murder of members of Param's pod had made its way around the ocean, as news of the death of every precious Master did. What rallied the formation of this super-pod was the fresh news that Orcas and Humans, the only two true predators, had very recently and quite cooperatively rediscovered an ancient power.

Param and the others had worked out as observers what Brough had missed as a participant. That is, his powerful closely scanning echolocation of the event was actually facilitating it. Simply turning off the echo scan, was not sufficient, as the Orcas had demonstrated they could achieve lesser, but still threatening results without a Master's full-scan echolocation. Param knew an attack on the Orcas, while not unheard of, would result in serious injury and quite possibly death to at least one of them. As the eldest of the Aware, her decision held—even one Master death was too great a risk at this early stage. Their numbers had taken a beating over the last several decades, and each soul was a vital part of their collective being.

The four Aware Masters agreed with each other completely in every detail they examined. The next strokes were risky. It required very close proximity to Orcas. They all concurred that Brough would be the one to go forward. He held the most detail up to that point. All Masters were taught by their first scanning games—everything means something. At this point, attention to everything was critical. Brough was satisfied that he had been chosen. He endeavored to learn absolutely all about his beloved ocean world and this was truly going to be the lesson of a lifetime.

# CHAPTER NINE

## Human: DELORA and LIAM

Delora woke up with the sun the next morning having enjoyed the deepest sleep of her life. She felt absolutely energized and positive. She stretched out, feeling acutely aware of the presence of all of her muscles. Before she even opened her eyes she could feel Liam propped up on his elbow in bed beside her, his stare boring a hole through her head. She blinked her eyes open.

"I didn't want to wake you." Liam's face was serious and he was already fully awake.

"Don't' worry, I'm awake. You look worried. What's the matter?" Much of that fantastic feeling softly popped away. She was back in her life, and recalled summarily all of its complications and demands.

"I'm lost, Delora. I used to know what reality was—at least I thought I did. Not anymore." He lay back down, staring straight up at the ceiling and they were silent for a minute. Liam turned his head toward her. "Today, out on the open sea, right?"

"Yes," Delora responded simply and stared straight up also. She knew without asking he was referring to the appointment Akenehi had requested, confirming virtually wordlessly that the dream-talk had indeed taken place.

Liam propped up again on the same elbow. "That was really weird being in your head, Delora. I thought somehow that if we could ever merge minds it would be fantastic. Now, I just feel…well, weird."

"Who asked you to join in?" she retorted sharply. "Do you think I did? I was just lying here with my eyes closed, drifting off, minding my own business, suddenly I was with Akenehi and then suddenly again, there *you* were, standing in the shadows, interfering with my Orca."

Liam drew back. "What? *Your* Orca? Okay, hold on. Do you think she would agree with that? She's no more yours than you are hers. Geez, woman, those sci-fi movies got it right, sharing minds is painful. Let me be clear, I don't feel weird because your *thoughts* were weird. I feel....*way* out of my comfort zone. Seriously, I don't think our species is up for this."

"Agreed. But it was good...except for the waking up part," Delora muttered the last to herself.

"Yes, but I was just thinking...I'm not sure we should go out there anymore. Hell, I'm not sure I can conceal my own thoughts around them after last night. We have to have some sort of defense."

Despite her initial annoyance at his interference, she found herself appreciating his input and even agreed with him. "We aren't in control," Delora considered slowly. "That's mostly it, isn't it? We're human, the masters of technology in our powerful boat with our symbol of scientific superiority, our C-cage, and she's supposed to be an ignorant, albeit interesting, animal. I'm not getting that anymore."

"Why do you think she wants us to go out there and find a sperm whale? You think maybe it was just a weird dream thing? You think maybe she wants to eat it?"

Delora hadn't gotten any feel from Akenehi whatsoever about the purpose other than a strong desire to *improve*. "I don't know if it's meant somehow to improve our communication, or what."

"Remember, she's not a natural liar. In truth, she may not be capable of it, nor feel she should deceive us. She really wants this and she expects us to comply."

She nodded. "Well, what's your gut feeling?"

"I'm out of my mind with curiosity. You? Now that I've seen through her eyes, it's a total game changer."

"I feel the same. Even if we find a whale, we can't make it do anything. It would swim away if it felt threatened, right?"

"True enough. Then I guess we are pioneers in spirit, after all. Into the wild, the unknown. But first..."

The both spoke the word in unison.

"*Coffee*!"

Liam made a better pot of coffee and he rose out of bed to begin brewing. "Eggs and toast sound good?"

"Perfect. And bacon." Then Delora reconsidered. "On second thought, skip the bacon. I don't want anything that heavy out on the water today. Besides, I think I'm finally going to be able to give up meat after last night."

"Yeah." Liam stopped in his tracks, grimaced, and reflected deeply. "All that blood and death. They love it, but frankly, it made me ill. Good thinking."

They both stopped talking for the rest of the meal preparation, because they each continued to quietly relive many of the shared thoughts of the sleep song. Before they sat down to breakfast, they heard a knock on the door. There stood Johnny in an obvious state of excitement.

"Guys! Glad I didn't wake you up. Can I go out to the Orcas with you today?"

Delora and Liam looked at each other with knitted brows.

"No," Delora stated simply. "Too dangerous. Why?"

Johnny began to hurriedly tell them how he'd had multiple inspirations lately, so many ideas about music and Orcas that he just had to get out there. He was finally figuring out he wanted to do with his life, thanks to them. He flattered them honestly saying they were role models and he wanted to learn everything he could from them. They'd faced the danger and they were fine, so why couldn't he help them and learn in the process? Oh, and could he use Delora's recording equipment?

Delora and Liam did not assume that Johnny was experiencing anything other than an enthusiasm which they themselves shared and encouraged about the Orcas.

Delora and Liam didn't even have to exchange glances to be in agreement not to tell him about Akenehi's subliminal request. They didn't want him going out on his own or with anyone else either. Their reasoning for that would be more difficult to explain and enforce. They were not the only people with a boat.

Liam thought quickly. "Glad to hear you're finding something that you're so obviously interested in. Imitation *is* a compliment. Thanks!"

Delora nodded in agreement but said nothing.

"But…" he offered, "We've already got something else planned for today."

Johnny deflated and looked ready to argue.

Liam quickly continued, "Why don't we make it a great trip next time out? We could plan well in advance. That would work much better for us and I *promise* we'll make it worth your wait. Good enough?" Johnny agreed reluctantly but firmly said he'd hold them to it. Regaining his full initial enthusiasm he left.

Immediately after Johnny left and the door was firmly closed behind him, Delora and Liam exploded into motion. Breakfast was forgotten as they made a list of gear to check, reviewed a protocol and decided on underwater hand signals.

* * * * *

To their amazement, there were reports of several sightings of sperm whales on the radio as they headed out to sea. They interpreted the news as confirmation everything was going well and as planned. They of course couldn't bring a sperm whale to Akenehi but they could certainly get as close as possible if they sighted one. They didn't.

They had prepared for the day's appointment with Akenehi by carefully considering many scenarios, options and outcomes. Delora had insisted on synchronized clocks, one was Liam's watch worn in the water and the other was to remain on the boat. They rehearsed hand signals to either continue or abort any activity once in the water. They geared up and waited eagerly for their date to show up. They reviewed their pre-choreographed steps as if practicing a wedding waltz; they felt the rhythm, pounding in energizing time with their hearts and both involuntarily moved in synch to it.

They then picked up the signals of familiar harmonized vocals as the Orcas approached, announcing they were not to be stood up. Akenehi was accompanied by only a few members of her clan. They circled a friendly distance around Delora and Liam, who held hands and gently maintained a depth of about five meters below the surface. The Orca vocalizations sounded a bit familiar to them. It would not have been the case before the sleep song. They enjoyed the complexity and the energy of the sound in context of the echolocation bursts, and it reminded them both of rock and roll, pop, and even classical music in the mix. Rather than experiencing fear, they were enjoying themselves immensely. Having decided on a few hand signals, including squeezes, to signal a desire to withdraw in the event of fear or doubt, neither of them picked up any vibe of anger or aggression, so they remained submerged. Through face masks they looked into each other's eyes, both were smiling, and Delora gave Liam the hand squeeze signal for positive feelings—three strong pulses in succession. He returned it.

Unmistakably excited Orca vocalizations and echolocation bursts rattled their masks and skulls. The music slowed its tempo until all hung still, as if vibration and sound itself had made a suspension net around it.

One moment Delora and Liam were surrounded by noisy Orcas, and the next moment they were suspended in the middle of what appeared to be empty space; water, ceiling, walls and floor absent. Tiny star-like points forming constellations of pentagons and hexagons encircled them. After they overcame their disorientation at the novelty of the surroundings there was simply no time to experiment with an ability to move or even to speak, because in the next moment they were back in the water watching the Orcas surface in unison.

Delora signaled to Liam. They had anticipated the possibility that sleep song could be a regular way to communicate with Akenehi, or perhaps any Orca. He held on to her and gently treaded water to maintain their present position. Delora inhaled a few deep relaxing breaths, concentrated on lowering her heart rate and relaxed her body until she felt herself naturally curl into a slight fetal position. She knew as long as her eyes were closed she would be in the initial alpha phase of sleep. That was when she had communicated with Akenehi before, and she hoped it would work now. She closed her eyes and concentrated on reaching out to the Orcas.

Their communication was successful.

When they got to the surface, back on the boat, Delora and Liam did not speak to each other. As part of the experiment they decided they would not discuss the events immediately with each other, but rather independently record in writing what had happened so as to eliminate influencing each other's recollection. Then they read each other's descriptions before they powered up the boat to return home. They had indeed experienced the same perceptions. Delora had included in her journal a cryptic, shorthand description of their second sleep song with Akenehi, as she realized this aspect of her research was purely subjective, aside from Liam's participation and experience. If anyone other than Liam read what she was writing that day, it would likely be met with total skepticism and even ridicule. Yet it was an important part of what was going on, and she felt she had to include consideration of all aspects of the experience.

There was no time difference between the synchronized clocks. Wherever they went time had passed equally. This suggested to both they had not traveled to any distance place. They had not been cognizant of being transported during their brief visit, let alone any sensation of adjustment to another time frame. Of course, it was possible, Liam offered, that his watch might have temporarily stopped functioning due to the powerful echolocation or some other effect. Delora acknowledged there could be explanations, but her heart pounded with exhilaration. She hypothesized although they perceived normal time passing for events, had they stayed longer a time difference could have been achieved. She was not discouraged by any means. She felt closer to time travel and to her son. They both knew extraordinary things were going to continue to happen.

**Orca: AKENEHI**

Change of plans, again. The humans had taught Akenehi in their first sleep song that they were experiencing something quite different than she and her family had practiced and intended. What Delora had conveyed to her was absolutely fascinating in its own right. Akenehi gave strict instructions to the small group that circled Delora and Liam (she had learned their human names from the sleep song and used them in her own thoughts from that point forward) that they were to sustain the song just as they had perfected it and then...simply watch and learn what would happen.

With luck, a long jaw would be present, there seemed to be a bloom of them very recently, and if assisted by those fearsome blasts, they might accomplish truly novel and exceedingly useful feats. There was the unfortunate chance the outcome would be Delora and Liam combined permanently into one creature, or worse. Despite her deep fondness for Delora, Akenehi was deathly determined to ensure the survival of her own kind at almost any sacrifice, including herself. Had not Delora and Liam requested more and therefore consented?

Akenehi located Delora's boat, as anticipated. Both humans were already in the water when they approached and were determined upon initial scan to be completely without fear. Directly below, to Akenehi's delight but not to her surprise, two mature sperm whales were deep enough so as to be safe from pursuit. They would not have been threatened by Orca even if they had come up closer. Akenehi wished they would come closer. They gave the whales enticement to heavily echo-blast. The Orcas sang perfectly. Akenehi observed intently as all vocalized, waiting for whatever was coming.

Then, Delora and Liam were suddenly...gone. The Orca's prior trials had sometimes resulted in a changed fish, but it instantly occurred. For the first time, something had disappeared off their radar; not swallowed and eaten, just suddenly gone. This was totally new to Orca concept. They all stopped singing after a couple of seconds out of sheer shock and surprise, and went into absolute silent stealth, as if an unseen monstrous predator had just revealed itself, threatening to devour them. Then Delora and Liam were there again. The Orcas had endeavored for something amazing, but how could they tell the rest of the clan about this? There were no whistles or clicks that meant vanish.

The Orcas present immediately broke formation and rose for a deep breath. Like Delora and Liam, they also had plans and signals for the coming trial. They followed their pre-determined protocol. They submerged and scanned their subjects and determined they were not dead, heartbeats were elevated but definitely there, and no changes were apparent even after further repeated scans. They summarized the lesson as two humans could safely be swallowed behind very dense teeth, then return in their original form.

Akenehi recognized instantly Delora's invitation for an at-the-moment sleep song, and they communicated sufficiently. Her dear one was truly an amazing creature. Akenehi was pleased Delora did not die. She determined from Delora's perspective what had happened. The Orcas had completed this important phase and could now continue planning how to proceed to the next. She would make the journey, to wherever they had gone at the first opportunity. Maybe there was hope for her family's survival after all.

### Sperm Whale: BROUGH and PARAM

Param and Brough had kept careful, stealthy track of the Orca group that was understood to pose the only threat for now. Param knew the Orcas had detected them, although they acted as if they hadn't. It was an old Orca hunting maneuver and she was not fooled. She and Brough, positioned directly below the small pod of Orcas and two confusing humans, commenced heavy echolocation straight up. The Orcas began their song and the humans swayed and rejoiced among them. They had calculated their echoes would have a specific result, unprecedented in recent scanned history, and they were perfectly correct.

A truly mind-bending series of detailed echoes returned to them. Param now understood Brough's inexplicable appreciation of the attractive power of the entire event sequence. She confirmed the seemingly impossible. One sacred microscopic bit had appeared between the humans as if the ocean itself had spontaneously given birth to it. The humans were there, and then the returning echoes where they had been became…interesting. They'd vanished. Several returning echoes completely confirmed it. And then they were there again, unmistakably as they had been. It was all recorded in the scans of two Aware Masters; there was no error.

Of course, this was not the first time the sacred bit had revealed its power and mystery in a Master's presence. Prior experience in the long past resulted in an Aware Master's ability to perceive them in the first place. For the past ten years, Param and a few distinguished others had been analyzing subtle indicators readable in the very energy of the ocean itself that an event was about to occur. In human scientific terms, they had detected an advanced wave. An event in the future that is of such a nature that time waves are sent to the past, which incidentally were readable by Param. As time for the event approached, the data in the wave became more dense and readable. Param knew with absolute certainty advanced wave zero was imminent. As the occurrence of the event approached, it was becoming clearer to Param that sacred bits would be involved.

*Four* had suddenly begun to make sense; one sperm whale, one orca and *two* humans.

Upon witnessing the human's disappearance and subsequent reappearance, Param was elated. Her scans revealed the advanced wave was still present and increasing in power, so the major event had not yet occurred, but would relatively soon. She shared her read with Brough and they swam off to celebrate what was left of the best day of their long-lived lives. They summoned the super-pod closer together into a dense, safe meeting formation. The results of the clicks were shared and committed to memory by all members of the super-pod. It was a glorious, memorable day.

# CHAPTER TEN

## Human: DELORA and LIAM

As soon as she was able, upon their return to dry land and home, Delora went into her sunroom, closed the door for privacy, opened her laptop and resumed dictating her experience in fuller detail as quickly and as clearly as she could. She was beginning the momentous task of explaining it all without sounding like an idiot. She was still trembling so hard she couldn't type. Computer transcribed rambling was going to have to suffice for now, stopped periodically until her voice stopped shaking. She massaged and shook her hands out and took a very deep breath. Liam was in the living room and she could hear him reading back his descriptions, struggling to find words to explain the day's events.

Delora spoke her sentences out loud, imagining she was just casually talking to Alvar. It helped her immensely.

**Delora's Journal**: *I think I experienced an anomaly in the expansion of our universe today.*

She played it back. *Oh God, that sounds so stupid*, she admonished herself. She shrugged helplessly then continued.

**Delora's Journal (continued):** *Space expansion occurs everywhere, all at once, at essentially the same moment. I don't know if the universes really* *expand or not. If they do, at least, if ours does, I sure never perceived it before. Maybe the expansion is not uniform. Maybe something can interfere with a certain expansion rate at a certain time. Maybe it can vary in certain locations within the universe. Maybe the expansion of the universe actually creates time. It carries everything with it from one expansion point to another. I don't know exactly what happened today, but something sure as hell happened. I have a witness, Liam McIlroy, who was with me. He is recording his experience separately right now as I speak. I'm sure he can confirm everything.*

*Somehow, I was able to remain at one size while the space me around continued to expand, and it put me in a bubble. I experienced it while remaining conscious; my own size felt normal, and Liam was the same size as me, the whole time, although we didn't actually measure each other, but he looked the same, pretty much the same, I think. I can't say I noticed if I was reduced compared to things outside the bubble, but I could see fuzzy stars all around us. They were the points of hexagons and pentagons. It looked like I was inside Alvar's C-cage. But it looked different from the inside. There was no metal structure but there were points, like stars. It happened at a rate so fast; one moment things were normal, then the next they weren't. I guess, assuming I'm correct; maybe we were stuck in a molecule. Yes, molecules in a molecule. I did some quick internet research and apparently those molecules can shrink-wrap smaller things, so maybe somehow my size was shrunk then held constant. That molecule just swallowed me up. But I lived. I came back...I think. Things were happening because time passed. Well, maybe I died. If this is death...but it feels just like life...so then how would I know I died? So where is Alvar then?*

She started laughing at that point. She decided it was time to stop dictating. She carried her electronics back to the living room in exasperation. "This is impossible. I'm babbling. No one is going to believe this."

"I'm sure your nonsense sounds just as plausible as mine. Listen to this: *The physical proximity of an organic being to a qualifying non-expanding sustained quantum event results in a physical entrapment of the organisms into a measurable "holding" area which lasts long enough for thought and even some decision making and allows some kind of transport briefly to what I believe is another time, dimension or perhaps another universe.*" Liam leaned back.

Delora screwed up her face and shook her head at him. "Another universe? Is that what you think happened? We went to a parallel universe or something? No, we shrunk and time travelled, I'm sure of it."

"How can you be sure? The clocks were the same!" Liam insisted. "Listen, let's be objective and believe not what we want to believe, but rationally think about the possibilities here."

"Were we overwhelmed by white noise, perhaps? Static? Were we stunned by the Orcas? No. I was rational and thinking and I was *not* in water. Liam, we were in that space with those constellations. We were in it. And I just know that if I had wanted to I could have..." But she stopped mid-sentence as she realized she had only remembered being at the center of perfect hexagon and pentagon constellations and nowhere else, and was indeed filling in blanks with a much desired conclusion.

"Yes, the constellations are consistent between your experience and mine. So that means we *saw stars.* Nothing more solid than that. Time travel may still be possible. I won't rule that out. But listen to how that sounds. Look at it." Liam pointed to one of their molecule models. "Can anyone believe we were in an object that size, let alone inside of a molecule, while still able to think and exist and then safely come back out again and live to tell about it? We are going to have to replicate this experience, prove to each other and ourselves we are not group-hallucinating or deluding ourselves, then let others in on this."

"Liam, no, absolutely not. Think of the consequences. I will not expose the pod to others in the context of something like this. You know I would rather die than see any of them taken captive. And really, what do you think happens next if we expose the pods ability here?" Delora stopped the conversation, realizing that the recordings they had just made were potentially dangerous to her beloved Akenehi. She erased hers immediately.

Liam watched her activity and understood her concern intuitively. He looked at her closely but he made no move to delete his own recording. "Do you want to do it again? Do you want to continue to document any of this? And if not, then what?"

"Yes, I do want to do it again. You?"

"Absolutely. It's weird but I feel great, not apprehensive or fearful in the least."

"Same here," Delora agreed. "I'm worried for the Orcas, what would happen to them if this got out, but not for us, not for this. I'm only sorry its pitch black out or I'd go right now."

"Lori, we need to record some of this. You know it, it's too big. What do you think about letting Johnny in on this?"

She blinked at him, consumed with putting the experience into words, so deep in thought she did not register that last suggestion. Subliminally she had heard it and an image of Johnny on the boat popped in her mind. The scene did not upset her. As she returned to her chair, she turned back to Liam to suggest it might be a good idea if they somehow informed Johnny. Liam, amused, said nothing but nodded in agreement. She sat back down and continued manually inputting her entry, more careful and thoughtful at her words.

**Delora's Journal:** *So we don't see ourselves or others expand like a balloon, even though I think anomalous space expansion occurred. Perhaps the Orcas have figured out a way to open a portal using a carbon-60 molecule, or its resonance shape; a method where they focus a series of harmonics that bounces around the water and pushes things into the configuration. It has wave properties and somehow the molecule and anything outside of it continues to expand at the rate constant with all around it—but the area inside, I don't know how far from the boundary, stops expanding, or slows, for a short, but measurable time in both human and Orca terms. What I am struggling to wrapping my head around is this—the universe expanding as one like a balloon but under certain circumstances part of it can get a "time out" from the expansion, which results in space/time alteration at that part and allows variation in expansion sizes/rates which could be measured relative to* *a basic unit of the expansion constant.*

*If I prepare for time travel being properly adjusted for "correct expansion size" I might be so small as to appear invisible to the current state of the universe, but would be properly sized to allow an instantaneous jump in time to the past. Indeed, an adjusted size compared to the current state might not even be detectable at even the atomic level. So it makes sense to me that we are able to travel forward in time because our physical bodies are "auto-adjusted"; carried passively along with the expansion. To halt even a piece of the universe from participating in the natural following of the flow and turn and "implode" back in an opposite direction may require an impossible amount of energy. Or not. Maybe once you figure it out it is simplicity itself. Like turning your head and heading back in the direction from which you came. So from an observer's perspective, wouldn't they see us shrink or if it happens really fast, just apparently "pop" out of existence?*

*Well, as far as successful time travel goes, then, we are also moving through space, around the sun and around the center of the milky way in intertwining spiral pathways, so in order to go back in time I would not only have to follow the exact trajectory or jump to the correct coordinates of the spiral backwards, but also adjust for the expansion of the universe between the two points in time. It seems impossible that any supercomputer would ever be able to correctly calculate each and every coordinate in space-time and therefore I will never be able to do it. No, I don't think it was time travel. Maybe Liam is right, maybe you can pop into another universe or dimension or something, but to physically transport a body we would have to come up with correct variables needed to calculate and then to execute the required implode and spiral backward so you transport to a safe location of your choosing without ending up being embedded in a concrete wall or have your head fused in the ceiling. Hell, maybe we just shrunk and that's it.*

*I'm thinking now that if I am to achieve actual time travel I will have to use methods other than physically transporting my body to a point in the past. Maybe I can just get a basic message such as, "Alvar! Don't fight! Go home now!" Since our physical bodies have the "wave" function and the carbon-60 molecules exhibit quantum behaviors and properties on a human perceptible scale there may be a way to utilize the ball and get a message to enter the "wave"—being everywhere at all points of space and time to communicate an idea. But if that works, then maybe some of the "feelings" or "gut instincts" I have experienced are in fact my future self or even past or future generations of time travelers who have achieved this method of communication. Maybe there is a proximity/ intensity relationship to the ideas and how far back an idea can travel. Instead of building a complicated apparatus, it may be a natural evolutionary development, like eyes from eye spots. The "universal oneness" can be tapped into as a sense and utilized to enhance survival. If successful, I can communicate an idea to myself to be in a certain place or time or make a suggestion to start or stop an event from happening. Yet how could I possibly pick out that message from the "white noise"? How can I guarantee that I will listen to that message? How will I stop myself from rationalizing it away?*

**Orca: AKENEHI**

Akenehi and the clan collectively studied the information they had gathered both from the event and the previous sleep song. They whistled and sang for hours on new insights into human emotion, priorities, and especially technology. The knowledge that humbled them all in Delora and Liam's presence from that moment forward were the images they had been able to obtain of the universe, its grandeur, beauty and variety. Up until the cosmic expanse conveyed by Delora, Akenehi had endeavored only to improve Orca bodies to increase hunting success in their current environment and provide better defense against land squid predators. Possibilities were emerging beyond her prior plans.

They sang ancient compositions; epic serenades of easy hunting with immense schools of prey Such imaginings becoming nothing more than that, myth and fantasy. The clans were all painfully cognizant of the decreasing amount of prey and the high mortality rates that recent generations were experiencing. None of them took it lightly or as unavoidable, and all felt urgency for their families.

Time travel, Delora's suggestion, was not on the Orca agenda. There was no need for it. It was a concept too unnatural. Orca kind was magnificent and their world was balanced in the past. It was the future that worried them, and they were headed there whether they liked it or not, that is, if they could survive it.

No, what the Orcas wanted was pure nature as they knew it. Now they imagined other ocean worlds existed which may contain an abundance of prey and might be therefore an Orca utopia where competition and land squid were nonexistent. The pod, like all other cetaceans, understood the changes in the appearance of the moon, corresponding with tides. But now they knew conclusively it was a world. As long as their bodies were in their current Orca-kind form, they would never directly experience it. She had felt Delora's envy and respect for her and she felt that was natural and to be expected. What she did not expect was to envy Delora from that moment forward, her ungainly, stiff, squid-like appendages, which she now knew had carried humankind to that place. It didn't take any of them long to imagine the results they had obtained that day could be as open water to other worlds.

Once they arrived at one of those worlds they could employ other newly acquired acoustic skills. Orcas, on their own, could now produce and manipulate adequate frequencies that resulted in successful, if not anticipated, wondrous bodily changes. Many of their experiments altering fish and other sea creatures had been wildly successful. Those successes were not sufficient. Through trial and error they determined that echolocation was not only helpful in directing the outcome, but an apparently necessary element for super-results. They had reached the upper limit of their own natural ability. Corresponding limits on precision and accuracy had been met. The pod also collectively realized that even with every excellent resource of Orca intelligence and natural ability it was still not enough. It would be dangerous to swim to such a world without a living, echo-blasting long jaw. They began to move in a direction unprecedented in Orca experience—to form a non-predator ongoing relationship with a long jaw to explore those possibilities.

But how? They could try sleep-singing, but long jaws didn't ever sing. It had never been attempted and Akenehi feared the fact that no love, therefore no enabling bond she recognized, existed between the Orca and long jaw. It made this idea unrealizable for her.

Once they located the long jaw and were being scanned by his echolocation they would give demonstrations, which did seem to work to a certain extent, assuming of course, they were not then attacked. Clever and curious as long jaws were known to be, how could one resist such wondrous novelty? An inspiration came to one of the males that they should mimic the long jaws click bursts so they might convey non-aggression. They all knew that was also a common tactic to lure them in during a hunt and would certainly be identified with a savvy older long jaw as a ruse and with that the idea was promptly chomped dead. One last detail was that they would begin after the next full meal so, when scanned, the long jaw would see they were completely and recently fed. That might give them more time to make their appeal.

**Sperm Whale: BROUGH and PARAM**

Like Humans and Orcas, Masters lived in a world of varying energy, from the planet's core to beyond the water surface. However, it was Aware Masters alone that possessed natural genetic ability to echo-scan read every detail, down to the molecular level, in their detectable surroundings. Because their ability had developed in a dense water environment, their abilities were virtually limitless. It would not be wrong to assume they could detect memory and data in the very essence of their universe. It follows that Masters had been privileged to a very special relationship with the universe; beyond respect, beyond affection, a relationship beyond a living brain's comprehension.

Every member of the super-pod was informed of the events. A new click series was shared among them and committed to memory, much like the "fish in a fish in a fish", a modified version was "sacred bit in a sacred bit". Teaching the young to become Aware Masters seemed to be a necessity after that day. They all marveled at the unseen yet powerful wonders of their world, and hypothesized with shared scan images what the coming event might be. Detection and recognition of this particular molecule was quite an advanced echolocation skill. It had taken Brough decades to learn to properly perceive them, and he did so only with the occasional tutoring and persistence by the eldest of the Masters, it had been one of the requirements to earn the designation "Aware". Param reproduced simplified clicks for the whole super-pod that enabled universal understanding.

As they began to comprehend, they wondered how a human could possibly possess knowledge of this shape. Maybe the Masters had underestimated humans. Perhaps, although they were like Orcas, dangerous murderers, they also had much in common with Masters in their ability to detect and appreciate the delicate and hidden qualities of their world.

And Orcas had the ability to produce the shape. Masters knew it held mysterious power and was linked to life and consciousness itself, and it terrified them to think that Orcas would create and control it. Brough shared his deepest concern that perhaps they had a new method of capturing their prey. A Masters size would no longer be an advantage against the Orcas. If the Orca's purpose that day was to display their ability, this was a deliberate demonstration for all Masters' knowledge. Their world had suddenly and permanently changed. Again, he became fearful. Param reminded him of their read of the advanced wave, increasing even now in undeniable power, which she could decipher more than any of them. Brough, also sensing to a lesser degree what was so obvious to Param, relaxed and became peaceful again.

## CHAPTER ELEVEN

### Human: DELORA

Alvar, expressing his love of hypothesizing, once told Delora that, in quantum reality, things seemingly pop into and out of this universe, duplications, mutations, and fluctuations of unimaginable creative power…otherwise known as—when weird things happened.

### Orca: AKENEHI

Akenehi, through her acoustic genius, had developed a sophisticated ability to produce quantum level events in her congruent Orca-sized reality. She didn't realize at the time what this meant, none did. Still, she was one of the most powerful natural beings in her universe of origin. She realized only her love for her family, her beautiful songs, and the storming desire to perfect the hunt.

She paused at the surface, having detected the characteristic echolocation vibrations she was hoping for, stopped and oriented towards the source. Perhaps the two young long jaws remained below because they perceived her non-aggressive intent. She quickly considered how she might invite them to remain and intensify their scanning with another harmonics demonstration. The clan had recently discovered a variation on the song that could hold fish smaller than a newborn Orca tooth suspended, although still alive. This was a seemingly inferior alternative to the usually stun method with a blast of echolocation, but it had entertainment value. They quickly assumed the correct harmonic formation and their vocalizations commenced. A suitable fish was quickly located, chased to center where it became trapped in place.

Sure enough, the scans from the long jaws below intensified.

The Orcas amplified and calibrated the harmonics of the song, intending to replicate the disappearance result obtained with Delora and Liam. Something quite unexpected occurred instead. Eight fish were suspended where one had been. They scanned and found them identical in every detail to the original fish, still alive and without injury. A larger fish was located, stunned, replicated and consumed.

Their acoustic power was unexpectedly greater than any relating to physical size and teeth. Orca worries for their family's survival were over.

Akenehi recovered from her amazement and realized the long jaws were leaving them, she assumed in terror, deep beyond her jaws and swimming away swiftly. Idiots.

Utilizing all communication channels, the clan conversed in whistle, echoes and a collective dream in sleep song, where they reviewed the series of events and especially the sudden appearance, ready to be eaten, of that first group of eight perfectly normal tasting fish. Many hypotheses were put forward as to why that result had not been observed before. They agreed it most likely had to do with novel variations in the intense sonar blasting of two rather than one long jaw.

Akenehi was impatient. If that demonstration did not draw the much needed echo blasts from a long jaw in for the length of time needed for proper experimentation she had no idea what would. It had never been attempted, as long as Akenehi could recall, a meeting or truce with any of the long jaws or even other dolphins or whales for that matter. The nature of the ocean was fish eating fish, Orca eating anything it desired, in waves of consumption. It was never questioned that there would be another way.

Having communed with Delora's alpha sleep, Akenehi saw method in interspecies cooperation rather than predation. She understood shared abilities lead to this new Orca acoustic technology. Orcas alone were too much a threat to long jaws. Excellent memory prohibited a long jaw likely dropping its defense, despite all their unaided efforts. Maybe Delora could be of use to her in forming a new kind of clan which included the long jaws. There were many uncertain and uncontrollable variables to consider.

Her family positioned her in their slipstream and calmed her with a favorite humorous song enjoyed when a clan member was in a mood they knew as "frustrated by persistent torrential rain". Her family knew just how to lift her spirits. She returned their affection and joyful displays. She loved them so very much.

### Sperm Whale: The Super-pod

Two young Masters, thrilled to be a part of the coming adventure, left the super-pod and went out on their own to scan for the Orcas. They were successful. Already somewhat vulnerable away from the large males, they were startled when they read their returning scans detailing the unprecedented, creative capability the Orcas had demonstrated. They expected to be delighted with a firsthand experience of the entirely new concept of *vanish.* They anticipated the excitement their return with additional details would evoke. What they received in their returned echoes, however, was quite different from anything they had learned from the elder's clicks. Eight fish where only one had been. They were pretty sure this was a completely different, albeit unprecedented, result. These two young Masters did not waste any time in rejoining their family and the elders of the super-pod that had remained scattered in the area. They conveyed the sonic imagery of the Orcas and their *procreating* multiple fish from a single creature.

Then the fearsome and wonderful consequences were projected among members of the pod in a cacophony of detailed clicks; so many they interfered with one another and made comprehension nearly impossible. In turns, scenarios were reviewed. Some rejoiced at the possible use for increasing the availability of their prey. Those ideas were quickly replaced with images of increased numbers of Orcas which, all agreed, would not be favorable in any way to Masters. Param read the intensifying advanced wave and its accompanying crests and valleys of memory that indicated the causing event was very close at tail; perhaps that night, perhaps tomorrow, but very soon. She clicked easy and content images and endeavored to erase all concern that mass death and disaster were at hand. It was difficult to convince them of the wave sensations they could not perceive themselves. Fortunately, a few other Aware also detected the same, and backed her up with confirming congruent clicks.

Unbeknownst to Akenehi, Orcas would not have to attempt to acquire a human mediator between Orca and long jaw. In fact, they did not have to execute any plans at all. The Aware were going to seek the humans out in earnest.

# CHAPTER TWELVE

## Human

Delora and Liam packed the boat with the usual gear and supplies and a few newly constructed C-cage models. As promised, Johnny was invited and he was overjoyed to be present. Liam sat him down once they were under way and briefed him. Liam and Delora would dive and he would stay on the boat and record any observations from there. Explaining to Johnny the concept of scientific control, Liam explained they did not want to taint his observations with suggestions on what to expect so they told him very little, except Orcas would be present during the dive. Delora placed a model around her neck on a rope, as was her habit when she was out on the water seeking the clan. At this point, they were not one hundred percent convinced they were necessary, but they weren't taking any chances. Liam ran Johnny through one final review of monitoring the recording equipment. Between Delora and Liam there was no fear, no doubt. They were ready and willing for a repeat experience. They hoped for an expanded one.

It was another beautiful, clear, brisk day. They were invigorated by the sunshine, the fine spray from the boat's wake and their rhythmic bouncing as the boat danced over each wave. They were heading out to sea, anticipating Orcas, specifically Akenehi and her clan. Delora was wild with anticipation that she would soon be in Alvar's living presence.

Instead of Orca, Delora spotted the distinctive blow of a sperm whale, the characteristic absence of a fin and then noted the blowhole off to the left of the head. She exclaimed and pointed to Liam.

"Liam! Johnny! Look over there. A sperm whale!" Delora was absolutely delighted. She always considered it good luck when she was able to catch a rare glimpse of this shy and extremely intelligent species of cetacean. "Oh my God, look at it. Beautiful!"

They cut the engine. She was amazed when the whale did not avoid her boat but rather came directly to it. She could clearly hear its heavy echolocation and she hoped it would find them non-aggressive, as they had nothing on the boat that would be associated with fishing or whaling. She picked up her camera and quickly took some shots of it blowing next to the boat, and lolling beside it looking up at her. Taking a quick estimation of the whale's size next to her boat, she concluded it must be a male. "Look, guys. He's *huge*." She noted several deep gash scars and also concluded quickly he was an older individual. He looked like he had survived many battles and surely enjoyed many giant squid dinners, despite the sharp beak slashing in self-defense.

"Here, before he goes away, lean over next to him and I'll get a shot of this." Liam and Johnny enthusiastically gripped the rail of the boat and leaned over a little. Delora had a gorgeous shot of the whale's large eye looking right up at her with Liam and Johnny smiling up at her in the foreground. She snapped a few shots in quick succession. "My turn!" She quickly traded places with Johnny. As Delora took position near the edge of the boat, very close to the whale now, she could not help but notice that whale's eye had followed her and was trained completely on the C-cage. She was too excited to pay much attention at first, she wanted this picture. She turned her head to Liam and smiled and leaned back a little, holding onto the railing, as Liam did, so she wouldn't tumble onto the whale. At that, the C-cage swung around her neck and dangled over her back, almost over the water.

Johnny took the shot. Liam had also noticed the whale was focused completely on the C-cage. . Liam traded places with Johnny and took one final image of the whale's clear focus. "Hey, Lori..." He slowly put the camera down. "I think he wants something." Delora turned and looked down into the whale's single huge expressive eye. He was still staring right at the C-cage. She slowly took it off the rope and gave it to Liam. "Liam, walk to the end of the boat. I'll stay here." The whale watched the model intently. Delora and Liam moved to make sure the whale was fixated on it. He was.

"Uh-oh," Delora anxiously realized, "I think Akenehi is on her way". She was filled with a moment's horror as she feared they may attack the whale.

As if he had understood her, the whale dove straight down under the boat and was out of her sight instantly. "Hope to see you again, my friend! Now get the hell out of here," she called to where the whale had been looking up at them just moments before. Liam quickly estimated the ocean floor depth and realized the whale was safe. They relaxed and got ready to greet the clan.

Delora guessed Akenehi had just barely missed that whale. The Orcas circled the boat excitedly. "Yes," Delora said to the familiarly marked fins, "there is a sperm whale close by." She pressed the playback recording of the greeting, following her usual protocol, then produced the human/Orca sound corresponding to C-cage. She placed the second ball in the net at the end of the wand and cast it out about seven meters from the boat. The increased vocalizations were the response she had anticipated. It seemed human and Orca were communicating successfully and her purpose was understood.

Delora and Liam were already in their gear and they only needed to make a few final checks and adjustments, then, giving Johnny and each other the thumbs up, they rolled backward into the water together. The Delora and Liam took their positions hovering about seven meters from the surface. They felt the familiar pulses of Orca and the strong pounding of sperm whale echolocation. Their masks rattled and their bones vibrated. It heightened their anticipation to exhilaration and near euphoria. They water-danced in natural rhythm to the cetacean's music. It could not be helped. The ocean itself carried them along in its joyful energy.

**Sperm Whale: BROUGH**

Brough and Param clicked the news the best case scenario was unfolding out to the super-pod. They had located and approached the vessel containing the sought after humans; who also had with them one of the very same large sacred shapes. Even better, they were within ultimate intense scan range.

As they had planned should the opportunity present itself, Param remained below and Brough went forward for close contact. Brough could not think of any other way to convey his interest to these humans rather than to show obvious focus. He surfaced in close proximity and looked directly at the humans who had obviously also detected him.

His vision was confirming what his detailed echolocation scan had identified as the correct boat, but also the inside contents and the location of everything, including Delora and Liam and the models. He had the object of his interest in his sight and now waited for any information on their intent. Nothing was happening. They were exchanging it between themselves and moving around, seemingly pointlessly, but the humans were not vocalizing. No, Brough thought. These creatures do not possess the ability the Orcas did.

He sent out a burst to survey the surroundings and was not surprised at all when his echoes returned the knowledge that the same small group of Orcas was bearing down on the boat. Fortunately there was enough time and plenty of depth below him and all he would have to do was dive deep to avoid a confrontation. He took a very deep breath.

Brough turned and oriented toward the Orcas' direction. He let out a loud volley of bursts with two-fold purpose. One, to scan the approach of the Orcas; and two, to coordinate clicks with Param. He heard her confirmation, deep but directly under him, the advanced wave origin was almost omnipresent. Whatever ocean-wide event was going to take place, it was imminent. The Orcas numbered only four, two adult females and two very large adult males, all with relatively full stomachs, but they were swimming fast and with purpose. Time to dive.

This is it, thought Brough. As he descended, his instinctive nature initially wanted to flee the area completely, but the data from Param, which he too was now able to detect with increasing clarity, indicated there was no reason to escape. He focused his echoes toward the boat where he guessed correctly the Orcas would engage the humans again. This was also such rare entertainment and learning, his instincts were easily subdued by his insatiable hunger for knowledge. He dove about one hundred fifty meters, far enough down to avoid the Orcas' teeth, but not their detection. Brough and Param had decided they could not attempt concealment; in fact, they were there to interact. The Orcas would know they were close, if they didn't already, as he began echolocation bursts which would not only observe the coming events but would convey them to Param and all the Masters within hearing distance. If he needed to dive further he could easily do so.

He hovered a distance above Param, in strategic locations for optimal echo reading, and directed his huge head toward the surface, swaying it back and forth, processing changes in return echoes. He didn't have to wait long as he scanned; the Orcas were quickly there, surrounding the boat containing the humans. Then the two humans were in the water. The Orcas did not attack. Rather, they sang, echolocated and moved with the turbulence of the water. Brough made his move, increasing with full decibel echo blasts as he ascended, increasing in speed as he moved his massive flukes in full power, then for reasons unknown to him, but originating in pure bliss, he rotated his body in accelerating spirals of euphoria, right up to the very center of the Orca arena.

**Orca: AKENEHI**

Akenehi detected the boat and the whale as if she were in sleep song. It was a surreal song of all hopes coming to subdued and tender prey, much sooner and more powerful than she anticipated. Delora presented them with the tuner as if Akenehi herself had delivered specific instructions. The Orcas began the perfected beautiful chorus, made flawless by the harmonics model. The clan fell into formation and did not break for breath or observation. Akenehi focused all of her vocal skill and acoustic intelligence into the resonance.

The Orcas could read Brough's approaching speed in their echoes, they could feel the pounding of the blasts. All but Akenehi adjusted their distance, so as to avoid a massive collision of flesh. It failed to intimidate Akenehi. Not only did she move in closer, she didn't even brace for it. The water's turbulence increased from amplified pure tones as well as moving massive Orca bodies and complex dancing limb and hand movement of the humans. Akenehi positioned herself between Brough below and the land squid directly above. She was the first Orca to produce the perfect harmonic. She amplified and synchronized the resonance perfectly with the rising bone-jarring echo blasts, which could only have been provided by the largest brained species on the planet, by a Master closing at deadly speed from below.

In less than a single click, less than an eye blink...a sustained quantum event occurred.

The event was created, in part, by an interaction of complex, powerful sperm whale echolocation bursts and the Orca produced carbon-60 molecule *mimicking* resonance. The effect was an anomaly which popped Delora, Liam, Akenehi and Brough instantly into subspace. All gear, water, inadvertent smaller lifeforms and matter in their immediate vicinity also snapped inward with them.

The instant that occurred, an *actual* carbon-60 molecule present in Liam's scuba gear's carbon filter with its own natural resonance was captured within the Orca produced resonance. The effect of that particular resonance within a self-similar resonance was unprecedented. A cage anomaly formed which further interacted dynamically with subspace. There, the resonances merged and boundaries became non-sequitur. The molecule also enclosed the mimicked resonance and this resulted in a creation event.

Brough, Akenehi, Delora and Liam were simultaneously transported and transformed into a unique state of being. They, along with all matter including smaller organic beings within that area, became "shrink-wrapped" inside the molecule, trapped but nonetheless alive and well. The properties of the carbon-60 molecule mandated they exist in both wave and particle state. The effect was such that all of those former beings, living, free-willed neurons of the universe of origin, were now combined in a particle/wave state of consciousness in their own brand new private universe. Chemistry, quantum physics and the presence of the humans, the Orca and the sperm whale provided most of the initial conditions. They were still uniquely themselves, yet simultaneously bonded into a single entity, so much more than a mere sum of the parts—they were the Vencello.

The Orcas had anticipated a specific effect. Akenehi believed, from their many trials, she might finally have full control and could perfect her physiology, separate her digits through the flesh of her pectoral fins to a new, superior Orca-kind that would possess arms and fingers which would help them prevent capture and improve hunting success. Orca-kind would produce at will a multitude of prey from a single individual. She might also swim to a new Orca utopia to populate with her family.

Delora had anticipated an effect. She believed she would be able to time travel; to send some kind of message back to herself or Alvar which would prevent his participation in that fatal encounter.

Liam had anticipated he would possess a permanent enhanced euphoria resulting from an increased experience of universal oneness and would be closer to Delora and experience Alvar's memory more deeply.

During and immediately after their joining, of the four, only Brough had his thoughts in order.

Brough had anticipated a significant advanced wave zero event would occur. Param had been correct. He was amazed not only that they were still alive, but that he was able to comprehend the read of his echolocation during the entire event. He understood he was in a separate place from Param and the super-pod. He recalled Param's clicks suggesting he communicate with her, although he did not know yet how that would be accomplished. He spent his first moments of solitary clarity processing his scan data.

One by one, the others began to regain their senses, awakening to their place in the dance, spinning and orbiting in each other's pull. It had begun.

## CHAPTER THIRTEEN

Meanwhile, back in the universe of origin, in normal space, a variety of perceptions had occurred. Johnny, alone on Delora and Liam's boat, recorded a cacophony of orca song, and visually observed Orca fins and turbulent water from the surface. He diligently monitored equipment but then turned it off and became concerned when the water quieted and the orcas dispersed. He became terrified, a coward's response, he admonished himself, when they did not resurface. He was horrified, convinced by the amount of violent turbulence and the Orcas that soon swam away, that his uncle and Delora had been injured or worse. He quickly realized that he might somehow be blamed for their injury or death if it had occurred. He was at another critical crossroads. It could be disaster but it could also be glory. He concluded this was the true hero's opportunity he had desired.

Akenehi's clan was elated with their success, which quickly dissolved into worry when she did not instantly reappear. They ceased all harmonics and even that did not bring her back. The loss of their beloved matriarch would be a catastrophe they were not willing to suffer. In haste, they spread out to examine a wider area in confused whistles, proclaiming that she would return somehow and call out to them, so shouldn't they remain quiet, and be vigilant for her, as she would surely rejoin them?

Param scanned the event in apprehension then relief that advanced wave zero had passed, the grandmother Orca, the confounding humans, and Brough all vanished as expected. She remained at ocean bottom even after the remaining Orcas left, scanning upward for evidence of his communications, or unexpected but highly anticipated return. It was during this time she read the ocean and understood an event at a separate location had occurred simultaneously at advanced wave zero. To her dismay, it was deeper than she or any Master could dive. She knew where she had to go, and to which to species she would have to appeal. Deepers. This wasn't going to be easy, even for her.

## ABOUT THE AUTHOR

As a university undergraduate S. Amaranthine had the privilege of befriending two cetaceans. The debut trilogy is born from those memories, a tribute to them with loving respect and admiration for their families.
S. Amaranthine holds a bachelor's degree in Psychology and a master's degree in Health Education.
The Vencello, first of a trilogy, is S. Amaranthine's debut sci-fi fantasy novel. Cetapiens is planned for July 2015 ebook publication with the third, Orcasekai, planned for December 2015.

www.ingramcontent.com/pod-product-compliance
Lightning Source LLC
Chambersburg PA
CBHW072001170626
46813CB00005B/1954

* 9 7 8 0 9 9 6 3 2 2 9 2 8 *